CHILDREN'S STORIES

in

DUAL LANGUAGE

GERMAN & ENGLISH

Raise your child to be bilingual in German and English + Audio Download

Ideal for kids ages 7-12

No part of this book including the audio material may be copied, reproduced, transmitted, or distributed in any form without prior written permission of the author. For permission requests, write to support@mydailygerman.com.

Table of Contents

Introduction

Hello, young reader!

Are you ready to go on a fun reading adventure? Reading stories is already a magical activity on its own. But do you know what's even better? When the stories also help you learn a new language.

Well, this book can do just that. Super cool, right?

In this amazing book, you will find ten short stories that will:

- Take you on exciting adventures
- Help you become better at understanding English and German
- Teach you to be a better listener with the narrated versions of the stories.

So, get ready to meet magical new characters and prepare to go on exciting quests.

Ready for your adventure? Turn the page and let's begin!

A Foreword for Parents

Congratulations on getting this book! Raising your kid to be bilingual is not an easy task. Buying this book, however, is one of the first steps you can take to help you towards that goal.

So, what exactly can you expect from this book?

- **You'll find ten different stories designed to be read by kids from ages 7 to 12.** Featuring a wide array of fun themes touching on dreams, quests, magic, and fantasy, you can rest assured that the material in this book is suitable for children and is appropriate for your child's age.
- **The stories are written in parallel text.** Each paragraph is written in both German and English — first in German, then in English. You can also read the stories in German only or in English only.
- **There is free audio material provided with this book.** You can access the audio at the end of the book. There are two audio files available: one in English, narrated by a native English speaker, and another in German, narrated by a native German speaker. The audio is designed to be a perfect supplement to help readers learn the correct pronunciation and improve their listening skills as well.

This book is suitable for your children, but the best part is you can enjoy it, too! Whether you want to improve your German (or English) as well, or you are simply in it for the joy of reading a story, this book is also great for adults.

So, enjoy this with your children or on your own — either way, you are surely in for a great time!

Thank you,

My Daily German Team

PLEASE READ!

The link to download the audio files is available at the end of this book. (Page 111)

Geschichte 1: Amandine & Der Zauberwald

Story 1: Amandine & The Imaginary Forest

Amandine's Wecker hatte gerade geklingelt. Wie jeden Montag stieg Amandine mit zugeschnürter Kehle aus dem Bett. Montag war immer ein unangenehmer Tag für Amandine. Sie wollte sonntags nicht ins Bett. Montag war Vortragstag.

Amandine's alarm clock had just rung. Like all Mondays, Amandine got out of bed with a tight throat. Monday was a strange day for Amandine. She didn't want to sleep Sunday night. Monday was recitation day.

Ihre Mutter, die sah, dass die Zeit knapp war, rief,

Her mom, seeing that time was short, shouted,

"Amandine! Beeil dich und iss dein Frühstück auf, wir kommen zu spät!"

"Amandine! Hurry up and finish your breakfast, we are going to be late!"

Amandine antwortete, ohne nachzudenken,

Amandine answered without thinking,

«Ja, Mama »

"Yes, Mom."

Sie beeilte sich und ging zu ihrer Mutter, die im Auto auf sie wartete. Amandine kam rechtzeitig. Sie war schon bald dran. Der Schüler vor ihr war gerade fertig geworden.

She hurried and joined her mother who was waiting for her in the car. Amandine arrived on time. It was soon her turn. The student who went before her had just finished.

"Sehr gut, mein lieber Antoine 20/20", sagte Herr Moulinot der Schuldirektor.

"Very good my dear Antoine, 20/20!" said Mr. Moulinot, his schoolmaster.

"Amandine jetzt bist du dran!"

"Amandine, it is your turn!"

Zitternd begann sie ihr Gedicht vorzulesen.

Trembling all over, she started to recite her poem.

„Die Krähe und der Fuchs. Herr Fuchs, ähm Krähe! Saßen auf ihrem Baum äh! Auf ihrem Baum saßen ... "

"The crow and the fox. Master fox, um, crow! Perched on their tree, ah! On their tree perched…"

Nichts an ihrem Vortrag war richtig. Das Urteil war klar: 4/20. Amandine lernte nicht gerne. Sie dachte, was ist der Sinn daran sich all diese Geschichten zu merken?

Nothing about her recitation was right. The verdict was final: 4/20. Amandine did not like learning by heart. She thought to herself, what's the point in remembering all these stories?

Eines Tages lief sie mit schlechter Laune nach Hause und traf einen alten Mann, der einen langen und grauhaarigen Bart hatte.

One day, while she was walking home in a bad mood, she met an old man, his beard long and grizzled.

„Hi junge Dame! Warum bist du so traurig?"

"Hey young girl! Why are you so sad?"

„Ich mag keine Montage! Dann ist Vortragstag. Die Geschichten sind nichts als Lügen, Dinge, die es gar nicht gibt"

"I don't like Mondays! It's recitation day. The stories are nothing but lies, things that don't exist!"

Der alte Mann zuckte vor Überraschung zusammen.

The old man jumped in surprise.

„Aber schau mal! All diese Geschichten sind wunderbar und sie sind real!"

"But, look! All these stories are beautiful and they are real!"

„Das glaube ich dir nicht!"

"I don't believe you!"

„Das ist ein guter Witz."

"That's a good joke."

„Okay, dann beweise es mir. "

„Okay, prove it to me."

Der zauberhafte alte Mann ließ sich davon nicht beirren.

The wizardly old man didn't let it bother him.

„Es liegt an dir die Wahrheit zu erkennen, kleines Mädchen! Aber ich kann dir helfen. Hier ist eine magische Formel – sie wird dir helfen, selbst die Wahrheit zu erkennen!"

"It is for you to discover the truth, little girl! But I can help you. Here is a magical formula – it will enable you to discover the truth on your own!"

„Du machst Witze! "

"You are kidding me!"

Amandine wollte nicht an Magie glauben und ging weiter.

Amandine, who did not want to believe in magic, continued on her way.

„Wie du willst, Kleine."

"Have it your way, my dear."

Amandine kam zu Hause an. Sie ass ihren Snack und öffnete ihr Aufgabenbuch, um sich ihre Hausaufgaben anzusehen. Zu ihrer Überraschung stand eine Nachricht im Buch anstatt der Aufgaben. Es war wie ein Zauber. In goldenen Buchstaben stand dort geschrieben:

Amandine arrived at her place. Taking her snack, she opened her exercise book to check on her homework. To her surprise, a message had replaced it, as if by magic. Written in golden letters, it said:

Liebe Amandine, gehe in die Nähe des Sonnenaufgangs. Gehe nicht in die andere Richtung!! Nenne den Titel einer deiner Vorträge und sage Simsalabim! Dann atme. Unterschrieben von dem Zauberer.

Dear Amandine, put yourself near the sunrise. Don't get the direction wrong!! Give the title of one of your recitations and say Poof! Then breathe. Signed, The Magician.

Er hat mir bestimmt mein Aufgabenbuch geklaut, um das da reinzuschreiben, dachte sie. Wir werden sehen, was er morgen

Abend sagt! Aber sie sah ihn nicht wieder und die Monate vergingen.

He stole my exercise book to write in it, for sure, she thought to herself. We will see what he says tomorrow night! But she did not see him again and the months passed.

In der Zwischenzeit war sie umgezogen. In ihrem neuen Zimmer konnte sie von ihrem Schreibtisch den Sonnenaufgang sehen. An einem Sonntag versuchte Amandine wie immer ihren Vortrag zu lernen. Sie konnte es sich nicht merken.

In the meantime, she moved house. In her new bedroom, by chance, her desk looked out on the sunrise. One Sunday, Amandine tried, after a fashion, to learn her recitation. It did not come to her.

Frustriert schloss sie ihr Gedichtbuch.

Frustrated, she closed her book of poems.

„Ich habe genug! Glaubst du, die Magie kann mir dabei helfen? Ich lese den Grashüpfer und die Ameise und Simsalabim", sagte sie und seufzte verzweifelt.

"I've had enough! Do you believe that I will get there by magic? Read 'The Grasshopper and the Ant' and Poof!" she said, sighing with despair.

Verdammt! Amandine erkannte, dass sie die magische Formel gesagt hatte. Sie legte ihre Hand über ihren Mund und ihre Augen waren weit geöffnet. Ein paar Sekunden vergingen und sie wartete. Nichts passierte.

Dang it! Amandine realized that she had said the magical formula. She clapped her hands over her mouth, her eyes wide open. A few seconds passed, and she waited. Nothing happened.

Froh darüber, dass sie recht gehabt hatte, stand sie auf, um nach ein paar Süßigkeiten zu suchen. Als sie aus ihrem Zimmer gehen wollte, schrie sie leise auf. „Ich träume doch! ", sagte sie zu sich selbst. „Das ist unmöglich, grüne Mäuse gibt es doch gar nicht!"

Happy being right, she got up to look for some candies. As she was getting ready to go out, she let out a small cry of fear. I am dreaming! she said to herself, it is impossible, green mice don't exist!

Nein, sie träumte nicht. Vorsichtig öffnete sie die Tür ihres Zimmers und ging hinaus. Es war nicht mehr ihr Zuhause, sondern ein wunderbarer Wald stattdessen. Eine grüne Maus lief vor ihr auf dem Weg. Amandine nahm ihren Mut zusammen und entschied sich mit der Maus zu sprechen.

No, she was not dreaming. Very gently, she opened the door to her room and went out. It was no longer her home, but a magnificent forest in its place. A green mouse rummaged on the path in front of her. Plucking up courage, Amandine decided to talk to the mouse.

„Hallo Frau grüne Maus. Kannst du mir sagen, wo ich hier bin?"

"Hello, Mrs. Green Mouse. Can you tell me what this place is?"

Die grüne Maus, die krank aussah, antwortete ihr mit einer leisen Stimme.

The green mouse, who seemed poorly, responded to her in a tiny voice.

„Das ist doch der Zauberwald!"

"It is the imaginary forest, of course!"

„Was ist ein Zauberwald?"

"What is this imaginary forest?"

„Nun, das ist der Ort, an dem alle imaginären Wesen leben!"

"Well! It is the place where all imaginary beings live!"

Und mit diesen Worten raste ein starker und robuster Hase mit großer Geschwindigkeit an ihr vorbei, gefolgt von einer Schildkröte, die sich sehr langsam bewegte.

And with those words, a strong and robust hare passed by at great speed, followed by a tortoise who was moving very slowly.

„Das ist ja der Hase und die Schildkröte aus dem Gedichtl!", sagte Amandine.

"It's the hare and the tortoise from the fable!" said Amandine.

Zu ihrer Rechten schaute ein Fuchs in Richtung einer Baumkrone, wo eine pummelige Krähe mit einem Stück Käse im Schnabel hockte. Und dort drüben sprach eine Ameise mit einem Grashüpfer.

On her right, a fox looked towards the top of a tree where a chubby crow was perched with a piece of cheese in its beak. And over there, an ant and a grasshopper were talking.

„Sie sind alle hier, das ist wirklich außergewöhnlich! Aber Frau grüne Maus, warum bist du so krank, wenn hier doch alle anscheinend bei bester Gesundheit sind?"

"They are all here, it's extraordinary! But Mrs. Green Mouse, why are you so sick while everything else seems in perfect health?"

„Schau dir doch die Tiere an. Den Hasen, die Schildkröte, der Fuchs, die Krähe und alle anderen. Alles, worüber ihr in der Schule redet, sind sie. Niemand spricht mehr über die kleine grüne Maus. Und deswegen bin ich jetzt krank!"

"Look at those there, the hare, the tortoise, the fox, the crow, and all the others. All you talk about at your school is them. No one talks about the tiny green mouse anymore! And that's why I am sick right now!"

„Wirklich?"

"Really?!"

Die grüne Maus erklärt,

The green mouse exclaimed,

„Es stimmt! Wenn ihr meine Geschichte nicht weiterhin vortragt, werde ich verschwinden!"

"It's true! If you don't perform my story anymore, I will disappear!"

„Oh nein!"

"Oh my goodness!"

Amandine war völlig verwirrt. Sie verbrachte viel Zeit mit der Maus, besuchte den Märchenwald und traf all ihre Freunde aus den Märchen. Aber Amandine sagte sich selbst, dass sie nach Hause gehen sollte, denn ihre Eltern machten sich bestimmt schon Sorgen.

Amandine was turned completely upside down. She spent a lot of time with the mouse, visiting the imaginary forest and meeting all of her friends from the fables. But Amandine told herself that she should go back home because her parents might begin to worry.

Nach ihrer Rückkehr kam ihre Mutter plötzlich in ihr Zimmer.

Upon returning, her mother suddenly entered her room.

„Amandine? Ah, da bist du ja! Aber was machst du denn. Ich rufe dich schon seit einer halben Stunde. Das Essen ist fertig."

"Amandine? Ah, there you are! But what are you doing, I have been calling you for a quarter of an hour! Dinner is ready."

„Ähm, ja ja. Ich lerne noch mein Märchen und dann komme ich."

"Um, yes, yes, I am finishing learning my tale and then I'll come."

Von dem Tag an, seit Amandine wusste, das all die Geschichten wahr waren, lernte sie diese mit ganzem Herzen. Sehr überrascht davon gratulierten ihr ihre Eltern und der Schuldirektor Herr Moulinot. Montag war jetzt Amandine's Lieblingstag und sie sang voller Vorfreude ihre Geschichte, ehe sie zur Schule ging.

From that day on, knowing that all those stories were real, Amandine learned them by heart. Very surprised by this, her parents and the schoolmaster, Mr. Moulinot, congratulated her! Monday had become Amandine's favourite day, and she joyfully sang out her recitations before going to school.

Eines Tages wollte sie etwas überprüfen. Also sagte sie die Zauberformel...

One day, she wanted to check something. So she said the formula...

„Eine grüne Maus ... und Simsalabim", sagte sie und atmete aufgeregt.

"A green mouse...and Poof," she said, breathing excitedly.

Sie öffnete die Tür und schaute sich vorsichtig um und sah Frau grüne Maus in bester Gesundheit! Amandine hatte Erfolg gehabt. Erleichtert erzählte sie weiterhin ihre Geschichten und zitierte ihre Märchen nicht nur um sich selbst glücklich zu machen, sondern auch um sicherzugehen, dass diese kleine Welt auch weiterhin leben durfte.

She opened up the door, carefully looked around, and saw Mrs. Green Mouse in good health! Amandine had succeeded. Delighted, she continued tirelessly retelling her stories and reciting her tales, not just to make herself happy, but mostly to ensure that this little world could continue to live joyfully.

Geschichte 2: Helena Zieht Um

Story 2: Helena is Moving

Helena hat, seit sie geboren wurde, immer am selben Ort gewohnt. Sie ging hier in die Krippe, in den Kindergarten und jetzt in die Grundschule, alles in derselben Stadt. Sie hat viele nette Freunde, mit denen sie immer viel Spaß hat. Jeden Mittwochnachmittag treffen sie sich alle zum Spielen im Burgpark und am Samstag haben sie Tanzunterricht. Man kann sagen, für Helena ist das Leben schön. Ihre Eltern sind nett und sie hat einen kleinen Bruder, der jetzt zwei Jahre alt ist und mit dem sie oft viel Spaß hat.

Helena has lived in the same place since she was born. She went from the crib, to nursery school, and now primary school, all in the same town. She has a lot of very nice friends with whom she has fun with all the time. Every Wednesday afternoon, they all go together to play in the castle park and, on a Saturday, they have a dance class. One can say that, for Helena, life is beautiful. Her parents are very nice and, what's more, she has a little brother who is now two years old with whom she often has a lot of fun.

Letzte Woche ging sie in den Zoo und durfte Samantha und Melanie dazu einladen. Nächstes Wochenende wird sie Stephanie und Anabelle in den Asterix Park mitnehmen. Helenas Freunde bedeuten ihr alles. Zusammen erfinden sie Geschichten, bereiten sich auf Prüfungen vor und versuchen Jungs anzusprechen. Auch als sich Helena in Bastien verliebte, aber Angst hatte ihm das zu sagen. Ihre Freundinnen dachten sich einen Plan für Helena und Bastien aus, damit sie sich trafen. Helena wird sich immer daran erinnern, wie ihre Freundinnen Bastien schubsten, sodass er direkt neben ihr im Schulbus saß. Das Problem war, das Bastien eher Samantha mochte und da Samantha eine ihrer besten Freundinnen war, war es Helena egal.

Last week, they went to the zoo and she was allowed to invite Samantha and Melanie. Next weekend, Stephanie is going to take her and Anaelle to Asterix park. Helena's friends are her entire life. Together, they invent stories, prepare for exams, and try to chat up boys. Moreover, when Helena was keen on Bastien, but was afraid to tell him, her friends came up with a plan for Helena and Bastien to meet. Helena will always remember the time her friends had pushed Bastien so that he sat right beside Helena on the school bus. The problem was that Bastien was rather fond of Samantha and as Samantha was one of her best friends, Helena didn't care.

Was Helena am besten gefiel, waren die Geburtstagspartys am Sonntag. Es gab fast jeden Monat eine Party! An diesen Tagen spielten sie Verstecken und Monopoly, bauten Hütten im Garten und machten andere großartige Spiele im Freien. Helena und Samantha waren die besten beim Dosenwerfen. Und einmal durften sie bei Julie zu Hause zelten. Sie machten ein kleines Lagerfeuer mit ihrem Vater und dann erzählten sie sich so viele Geschichten, dass sie alle eine Gänsehaut bekamen.

What Helena liked the most was Sunday birthday parties. There was one almost a month! It was at those events that they had the best hide-and-seek games. They played Monopoly, with good pay, made huts in the garden, and other great outdoor games. Helena and Samantha were the strongest at Kick-the-Can. And one time, they were allowed to do some camping at Julie's place. They made a small campfire with her dad, and then they told many stories that gave them all goosebumps.

Aber eines Tages bemerkte Helena etwas Merkwürdiges bei ihr zu Hause. In der Garage fand sie Kartons, einer auf dem anderen gestapelt mit den Namen von Zimmern, Küche, Badezimmer und Geschirr (ACHTUNG ZERBRECHLICH!), Lucas Zimmer, Helenas Zimmer … usw.

But one day, Helena noticed something strange at her place. In the garage, she found boxes piled one on top of one another, some with the names of rooms, kitchen, bathroom, and dishes (ATTENTION FRAGILE!), Lucas's Room, Helena's Room…etc.

„Es ist merkwürdig oder?", sagte sie zu ihren Freundinnen. Dann, als die Tage vergingen, wurde das Haus immer leerer, bis zu dem Tag, an dem das Drama seinen Lauf nahm. Es war Samstag Nachmittag und anstatt mit ihren Freundinnen tanzen zu gehen, mussten Helena und ihr Bruder bei ihren Eltern bleiben, weil diese ihnen etwas mitteilen wollten. Die Neuigkeiten kamen wie ein Donnerschlag: Sie zogen um! Es war schrecklich!

"It's weird, don't you think?" she said to her friends. Then, as the days passed, she found the house was being emptied more, right up until the day the drama began. It was a Saturday afternoon, and instead of going dancing with her friends, Helena and her brother had to stay with their parents because they wanted to tell them something. The news came like a thunder strike: they were moving! It was dreadful!

Alles passierte so schnell. Helena hatte kaum Zeit, sich von ihren Freundinnen zu verabschieden. Sie versuchten Helena zu beruhigen. Dazu kam noch, dass der Umzug während der Sommerferien stattfand, genau die Zeit im Jahr, die sie am liebsten mit ihren Freundinnen verbrachte. Der Start im neuen Schuljahr war schwierig für Helena – sie kannte niemanden

dort. Da sie zum ersten Mal umgezogen war, wusste sie nicht, wie sie die Dinge angehen sollte. Oft versuchte sie sich zu integrieren, aber es half nichts. Eines Tages wollte eine Gruppe Jungs sie zum Fußballspielen auf dem Feld einladen. Sie zögerte. Erstens waren es Jungs und sie mochte keine Jungs. Zweitens und das war noch wichtiger, mochte sie gar kein Fußball. Sie vermisste bereits all die schönen Zeiten, die sie mit ihren alten Freundinnen hatte. Hier gab es keine Samantha, die den ganzen Tag Witze machte, keine Melanie, mit der sie Hüpfen spielen konnte und keine Anabelle, die Meisterin des Gummibands war!

Everything happened very quickly. Helena barely had time to say goodbye to her friends, who were trying to reassure her. On top of that, the move was taking place during the summer break, the time of year when she had the most fun with her friends! The start of the new school year was difficult for Helena — she did not know anyone there. As it was the first time she had moved, she did not know how to go about things. Many times, she tried to integrate, but to no avail. One day, a group of boys wanted to invite her to play football on the field. She hesitated. First, they were boys, and she didn't like boys. Second, and more importantly, she did not like football. She already missed all of the marvelous times she had had with her old friends. Here, there was no Samantha who made jokes all the time, no Melanie with whom she played hopscotch, and no Anaelle, the elastic champion!

Man kann aber nicht sagen, dass Helena nicht gewillt war. Ganz im Gegenteil. Sie verbrachte die meiste Zeit alleine, bis sich ihr eines Tages eine Möglichkeit bot. Eine Gruppe von Mädchen akzeptierte Helena in ihrer Clique. Sie waren zu viert und mit ihr jetzt zu fünft. Da waren Patty, die groß und stark

war, Christelle und Coralie, die Zwillinge waren und Nora, die klein, aber sehr schnell war.

You can't say that Helena was unwilling, though. Quite the contrary. She spent a lot of her time alone, until one day, an opportunity finally presented itself. A group of girls accepted Helena joining them! They were a group of four, and now five including her. There was Patty, who was tall and strong, Christelle and Coralie, who were twin sisters, and Nora, who was small but very fast.

Helena stimmte zu, obwohl es schon bald ein Problem gab. Ihre neuen Freundinnen waren echte Prankster – sie machten den ganzen Tag Streiche. Aber das machte ihr nichts aus. Helena hielt es einfach nicht mehr länger alleine aus! Was es auch immer war, sie musste mit den ersten Freunden, die sie gefunden hatte, gut auskommen. Und so fand Helena sich Schritt für Schritt mehr dazu verpflichtet, an den Streichen ihrer neuen Freunde teilzunehmen. Eines Tages musste sie das Waschbecken mit Toilettenpapier füllen und den Wasserhahn laufen lassen, sodass das Waschbecken überlief und eine Flut in der Mädchentoilette entstand. Sie war nicht stolz auf sich selbst, aber sie hatte keine andere Wahl. Ansonsten würde sie alle ihre neuen Freundinnen verlieren. Ein anderes Mal brachten sie sie dazu, während der Pause die ganze Tafel im Klassenzimmer abzuwischen. Dann brachten sie sie dazu, die Malertuben auszudrücken, Vivien's Stifte zu klauen und ihr Glas in der Cafeteria zu verschütten. So ging es weiter, bis Helena eines Tages auf frischer Tat erwischt wurde.

Helena accepted, although a problem soon presented itself. Her new friends were real pranksters — they fooled around all the time. But, never mind that. Helena could not stand to be all alone anymore! Whatever the cost, she had to get along well with the first friends she found. Just like that, little by little, Helena found herself obliged to participate in the pranks of her new friends. One day, she had to fill up the wash basin with toilet paper and leave the tap running so that the basin overflowed everywhere, creating a flood in the girls' bathroom! She was not at all proud of herself, but she did not have any other choice. Otherwise, she would lose all her friends. Another time, they got her to erase the entire chalkboard in the classroom during recess. Then, they got her to spill the paint tubes, to steal Vivien's pens, and knock over her glass in the cafeteria. It continued until, one day, Helena got caught red-handed.

Als sie gerade gegen ihren Willen Schimpfwörter an die Tafel schrieb, kam plötzlich Frau Hubert in das Klassenzimmer! Die Strafe kam sofort: Für eine Woche musste sie zweihundert

Mal am Tag den Verhaltenskodex der Schule abschreiben. Zusätzlich durfte Helena nicht rausgehen und auch fünfzehn Tage lang kein Fernsehen schauen! Keine ihrer Erklärung half ihr.

When she had to, against her will but she had to, write swear words on the chalkboard, Mrs. Hubert suddenly entered the classroom! The punishment was instantaneous: for one week, she had to copy two-hundred times per day the school's code of conduct. In addition, Helena was not allowed to go out, and she was not allowed to watch television for fifteen days! No explanation worked in her favor.

Helena hatte ihre Lektion gelernt. Es war besser, alleine zu sein als in schlechter Gesellschaft! Sie schwor sich, sich niemals mehr mit schlechten Menschen anzufreunden. Zum Glück fand Helena schnell neue Freunde, mit denen sie genauso viel Spaß hatte wie früher. Und das Beste daran war, dass Helena ein Jahr später all ihre Freunde im College wieder traf. Sie stellte ihre neuen Freunde ihren alten Freunden vor und zusammen waren sie ein wunderbares Tanzteam.

Helena learned her lesson. It was better to be all alone than to be with bad company! She swore to herself never to be friends with bad people ever again. Fortunately, Helena made some new friends very quickly and with whom she had fun with just as much as before. And the icing on the cake was when, one year later, Helena found all her friends again in college! She acquainted her new friends with her old friends and, together, they created a magnificent dance team.

Geschichte 3: Erwan & Die Musik Der Sphären

Story 3: Erwan & The Music of the Spheres

Erwan ist ein junger Mann, der normalerweise sehr neugierig ist, aber manchmal auch ein wenig faul. Er liest gerne, schreibt ab und zu, schaut Filme und hört gerne Musik. Er mag all Schulfächer – Geschichte, Mathe, Französisch. Es gibt jedoch eine Sache, die mehr heraussticht als alles andere. Erwan mag es nicht, wenn ihm jemand sagt, was er tun soll. Sobald er etwas tun muss, verliert er das Interesse. Das Problem ist, dass Erwan's Eltern unbedingt wollen, dass er klassische Musik spielt. Es ist wirklich blöd, denn er mag Musik wirklich, aber jetzt fühlt er sich dazu verpflichtet und daher mag er die Musik nicht mehr.

Erwan is a young boy who is usually curious, but also a bit lazy sometimes. He likes to read, write from time to time, watch movies, and listen to music. He is interested in all the subjects in school – history, math, French, everything. However, there is one thing he detests more than anything else. Erwan does not like to be told what to do. As soon as he is obliged to do something, he loses all interest in it. Now, the problem is that Erwan's parents desperately want him to play classical music. It is too bad, because he really liked music but now he feels obliged to do it, and therefore does not like it anymore.

Jedes Mal, wenn er zur Musikschule geht, ist es eine Tortur. Musiktheorie erscheint ihm schrecklich langweilig. Er fragt sich selbst, warum er das tun muss, warum er unbedingt Musik lernen muss. Dazu kommt noch, dass Herr Constant, der Musiklehrer, ihn überhaupt nicht mag. Er findet, dass Erwan besonders faul ist und er kein Interesse an musikalischer Erziehung hat. „Das stimmt nicht!" antwortete Erwan. „Im Gegenteil, ich bin jemand, der sehr neugierig ist, das weiß ich!", fügte er hinzu. Er konnte nichts tun. Eines Tages musste er als Strafe die ganze Partitur von "Au Clair de la Lune" nach dem

Unterricht abschreiben. Er hatte genug. Erwan wollte nicht mehr zur Musikschule gehen, aber er musste bis zum Ende des Semesters warten.

Each time he goes to the conservatory, it is like torture. Music theory seems terribly boring to him. He asks himself why he is obliged to do this, why he absolutely must learn music. To top it all off, Mr. Constant, the music teacher, does not like him at all. He finds, justifiably, that Erwan is particularly lazy and he does not voluntarily interest himself in musical education. "That's not true!" responded Erwan. "On the contrary, I am someone who is very curious, I know this!" he added. There was nothing to be done. One day, as a punishment, he had to write the entire score of "Au Clair de la Lune," right up until the end of class! He had had enough, Erwan did not want to go to the conservatory anymore, but he had to wait until the end of the term.

Am letzten Tag vor den Ferien wurde Erwan gefragt, welches Instrument er für den Start des Schuljahres wählen möchte. Völlig desinteressiert antwortete er wahllos:

„Klavier... ja, das Klavier ist eine gute Wahl!"

On the last day before the holidays, Erwan was asked what instrument he was going to choose for the start of the school year. Completely disinterested, he responded haphazardly,

"The piano ... yes, the piano is a good choice!"

Die Ferien gingen vorbei und nach seiner Rückkehr war Erwan wirklich entschlossen. Er war immer noch nicht an Musik interessiert, also würde er einfach Ende des Semesters gehen. Immerhin würde seine erste Stunde Klavierunterricht sein und er musste nicht mehr Herrn Constant zufriedenzustellen, weil er Violine unterrichten würde.

The holidays passed and, upon his return, Erwan was truly decided. He was still not interested in music, so he would leave at the end of the term. All the same, the first class would be his piano lesson, and he would not have to please Mr. Constant because he would be teaching violin.

Er kam an der Tür des Klavierzimmers an und klopfte. Er wartete ein paar Sekunden und trat dann ein. Der Raum war wunderschön mit beruhigenden und besänftigenden Bernsteinleuchten, ganz anders, als er sich vorgestellt hatte. Ein tolles schwarzes Klavier wartete auf ihn, es stand mitten im Zimmer auf einem wunderbaren Teppich. Sein Lehrer hieß ihn herzlich willkommen. Er war noch recht jung und hatte wunderschöne lange Haare. Er war sehr nett.

He arrived at the door of the piano room, knocked on the door, waited a few moments, and then entered. Contrary to what he had imagined, it was a very beautiful room with calming and soothing amber lights. A superb black piano waited for him, placed in the middle of the room on a magnificent carpet. His teacher welcomed him warmly. He was fairly young and had very beautiful long hair. He seemed very nice.

„Hallo, mein lieber Erwan. Ich bin Herr Serap. Du hast das Klavier gewählt, gute Wahl!"

"Hello, my dear Erwan. I am Mr. Sérap. You have chosen the piano, good choice!"

Erwan war ein wenig schüchtern.

Erwan was a little bit shy.

„Gut. Zum Anfang können wir uns ein wenig unterhalten, ehe wir mit dem Spielen beginnen, hört sich das gut an?"

"Good. To start, we will chat a little before we begin to play, does that sound good?"

Erwan stimmte zu. Dann begann der neue Lehrer ihm eine wunderbare Geschichte über die Ursprünge des Klaviers zu erzählen, seine Geschichte wie es erschaffen wurde und warum und was er damit tun konnte. Am ersten Tag berührte Erwan nicht eine Taste am Piano und auch am zweiten oder dritten Tag nicht. Er liebte es dorthin zu gehen – all die Geschichten, die Herr Serap erzählte, waren so interessant.

Erwan agreed. That is when his new teacher began to tell him an admirable story about the piano's origins, its history, how it was created and why, and what he could do with it! The first day, Erwan did not touch even one key on the piano nor on the second day, or the third. He loved to go – all the stories that Mr. Sérap told were so interesting.

Am siebten Tag ging Erwan wie üblich in das Klavierzimmer. Er ging hinein und zum ersten Mal sah er seinen Lehrer hinter dem schwarzen Klavier sitzen. Herr Serap bat Erwan sich neben ihn zu setzen.

On the seventh day, Erwan went as usual to the piano room. He went in and, for the first time, he saw his teacher seated behind the black piano. Mr. Sérap asked Erwan to sit beside him.

„Heute, mein lieber Erwan werden wir über die echte Geschichte sprechen, die Musik uns erzählt. Bist du bereit?"

"Today, my dear Erwan, we are going to talk about the true story that music continually tells us. Are you ready?"

„Auf jeden Fall! Aber wie kann Musik uns eine Geschichte erzählen, wenn sie gar keinen Mund hat", wunderte sich Erwan.

"Definitely! But how can music tell us a story if it doesn't have a mouth?" exclaimed Erwan.

„Lass dich nicht täuschen! Höre gut zu – deine Augen werden heute deine Ohren sein, okay?"

"Don't be mistaken! Open your ears wide – they will be your eyes today, okay?"

„Ja!" antwortete Erwan und wartete angespannt darauf, was sein Lehrer ihm zeigen würde.

"Yes!" responded Erwan, anxiously waiting to see what his teacher would present him with.

„Ich werde dir ein Geheimnis erzählen. Aber sei vorsichtig, ein Geheimnis ist heilig. Und alles, was heilig ist, ist verpflichtend", sagt Herr Serap lachend. „Ich mache Witze, behalte das Geheimnis für dich und erzähle es niemandem."

"I am going to tell you a secret. But be careful, a secret is sacred! And everything that is sacred, is binding!" said Mr. Sérap laughing. "I'm joking, keep the secret to yourself, and do not tell anyone."

„Versprochen", erwiderte Erwan.

"It's a promise!" said Erwan.

„Also dann, wusstest du, dass Musik, wenn sie gut gespielt wird, Sphären schafft?"

"Well then, did you know that music, while it's being played well, creates spheres?"

„Sphären?!" sagte Erwan erstaunt. „Ich habe noch nie Sphären gesehen, wenn ich Musik höre!"

"Spheres?!" said Erwan in amazement. "I have never seen spheres when listening to music!"

„Oh wirklich? Dann komm mal ein wenig näher und konzentriere dich."

"Oh yah? Well come a little bit closer and concentrate."

Erwan spitzte seine Ohren und lauschte, während Herr Serap ein Stück von Erik Satie spielte.

Erwan picked up his ears and listened while Mr. Sérap played a piece by Erik Satie.

„Das ist Gnosienne #1", flüsterte er leise, während er spielte.

"It is the Gnosienne #1," he whispered softly while playing.

„Ich sehe nichts!", bemerkte Erwan.

"I don't see anything!" Erwan remarked.

„Konzentriere dich ein wenig mehr. Du wirst sehen, es wird kommen..."

"Concentrate a little bit more. You will see, it will come..."

Also versuchte Erwan sich noch mehr zu konzentrieren. Er erlaubte sich selbst, die Musik in sich aufzunehmen und plötzlich dachte er, er sah eine kleine Sphäre aus dem Klavier kommen. Sie sah wie eine Seifenblase aus, in der sich die Farben spiegelten.

So Erwan tried his hardest to concentrate. He allowed himself to be absorbed by the music and, all of a sudden, he thought he saw a small sphere coming out of the piano. It resembled a soap bubble with reflecting colors.

„Wow! Das ist fantastisch! Was ist das?", fragte er.

"Wow! It's fantastic! What is it?" he asked.

„Das mein lieber Erwan, ist, was wir die Musik der Sphären nennen! Und weißt du, was wir damit machen können?"

"This, my dear Erwan, is what we call the Music of the Spheres! And do you know what we can do with it?"

„Nein", antwortete Erwan.

"No," responded Erwan.

„In diesen Sphären gibt es eine andere Welt, ein ganzes Universum, das du entdecken kannst."

"Inside one of these spheres, there is another world, an entire universe which you can explore."

„Wirklich?", fragte Erwan total verwundert.

"For real?" asked Erwan, totally amazed.

„Ja! Jedes Stück Musik hat seine eigene Sphäre, sein eigenes Universum!"

"Yes! Each piece of music has its own sphere, its own universe!"

„Und wie kommen wir dorthin?", wollte Erwan neugierig wissen.

"And how do we go there?" inquired Erwan curiously.

„Dafür ist es notwendig dass du selbst Musik machst!"

"For that, it is necessary to play the music yourself!"

„Dann muss ich auf jeden Fall Klavier spielen lernen!", sagte Erwan glücklich.

"Then I absolutely have to learn how to play the piano!" said Erwan happily.

Erwan übte so oft er konnte. Er lernte Musiknoten, Partituren, Theorien und das Klavier genau kennen. Er fand fast jeden Tag die Zeit zum Üben. Seine Eltern waren erleichtert und Herr

Constant ärgerte ihn nicht mehr. Eines Tages, nachdem er lange geübt hatte, setzte er sich an das Klavier im Musikzimmer, schloss seine Augen und begann zu spielen. Seine Hände glitten mühelos über die Klaviertasten und erzeugten eine prächtige Melodie. In dem Moment als er spielte, ohne nachzudenken, konnte er in die versteckte Welt der Sphäre eintreten, die von dem Klavier freigegeben wurde. Erwan konnte seinen Augen nicht trauen! Diese Welt war wunderbar, bewohnt mit zahlreichen Kreaturen, die normalerweise nur in Märchen vorkommen.

Erwan practiced as often as he could. He learned musical notes, scores, theory, and the piano. Almost every day he found time to practice. His parents were delighted and Mr. Constant did not bother him anymore. One day, after he had been practicing for a long time, he settled at the piano in the music room, closed his eyes, and started to play. His hands glided over the piano keys effortlessly, creating a sumptuous melody. In that moment, while he was playing without thinking, he was able to enter the hidden world in the sphere that was released from the piano. Erwan could not believe his eyes! This world was magnificent, inhabited by numerous creatures typically found in fairy tales.

Von dem Tag an übte Erwan Tag und Nacht und wurde einer der besten Musiker der Welt und natürlich eine der ersten Schriftsteller, der über Musik der Sphären schrieb, für die, die es natürlich erkennen konnten.

From that day on, Erwan trained night and day, becoming one of the best musicians in the world and, of course, one of the first writers of Music of the Spheres, for those who could recognize it, of course.

Geschichte 4: Chloe & Die Glückskarten

Story 4: Chloe & The Fortune Cards

Chloe ist schon immer ein sehr kluges Mädchen gewesen. Sie war ein Beispiel in allen Bereichen, egal ob Sport oder Grammatik, Chloe war und ist immer die Beste, das dachte sie zumindest! Obwohl Chloe sehr gut ist, gibt es eine Sache, die sie nicht so gut kann. Obwohl sie immer versuchte, das vor anderen zu verstecken, wurde es immer schwerer und schwerer. Chloe hat tatsächlich Angst vor der Zukunft. Es gefällt ihr nicht, nicht zu wissen, was mit ihr passiert. Ohne Zweifel ist das der Grund, warum Chloe immer die Beste war. Sie wusste nie, was passieren konnte und so plante und berechnete Chloe lieber alles. Aber je älter Chloe wurde und je mehr Dinge ihr passierten, umso schwerer fiel es ihr, Dinge vorauszusehen.

Chloe has always been a very bright girl. Exemplary in all areas, whether sports or grammar, Chloe is, and will always be, the best, such were her beliefs! Although Chloe is excellent, there is one thing she is not so talented at. While she has always tried to hide it from others, it has become more and more difficult. Chloe is actually afraid of the future, she doesn't like not knowing what will happen to her. Without a doubt, that is why Chloe has always been the best. Never knowing what could happen, Chloe preferred to plan and calculate everything. However, as Chloe gets older, and more and more things happen, it becomes very hard for her to anticipate everything.

Sie musste eine Lösung finden. Egal, ob es das Frühstück am Morgen, der Nachmittag in der Cafeteria oder das Essen am Abend war, Chloes Kopf arbeitete ununterbrochen. Sie hatte über alles nachgedacht, aber es war nichts dabei rausgekommen. Es war unmöglich, eine Idee zu finden, die sie retten würde und die Zeit lief. Eines Tages, als sie gerade mit ihren Eltern im Quartier Latin von Paris unterwegs war, wurde sie plötzlich auf etwas aufmerksam. Hinter einem Fenster, einer

sonderbaren Boutique mit nur ein paar Büchern darin, lag ein kleines Kartenspiel. Darunter waren die Worte geschrieben: "Die Zukunft macht dir Angst, du würdest gerne dein Schicksal erfahren und entdecken, was die Zukunft für dich bereit hält – dann ist dieses Spiel für dich und kostet nur 12 Euro!"

She had to find a solution. Whether it was in the morning at breakfast, in the afternoon in the cafeteria, or in the evening at dinner, Chloe racked her brains without stopping. She had thought of everything, but nothing came of it. It was impossible to find an idea that would save her and the clock was ticking. One day, while she was walking with her parents in the Latin Quarter of Paris, something caught her eye. Behind a window of a peculiar boutique, with only a few books in it, there lay on a small stand a game of cards. Underneath it were inscribed the words: "The future scares you, you would like to know your destiny and discover what your future holds for you –this game is for you, for only €12!"

Genau das brauchte sie. Nachdem sie mit ihren Eltern verhandelte, erhielt Chloe 12 Euro und kaufte sich das Kartenspiel. Sobald sie zu Hause war, schloss Chloe sich in ihr Zimmer ein und packte die Karten aus. Es waren nicht nur gewöhnliche Karten – nein, jede Karte hatte ein anderes Bild und eine römische Zahl darauf. Das war kein Problem für Chloe, die bis zur Zahl 29 in römischen Zahlen lesen konnte. Eine kleine Anleitung lag den Karten bei. So einfach war es nicht. Chloe musste die Bedeutung der Bilder lernen. Es gab alle Arten von Bildern – eine Sonne, ein Stern, ein Mond und es gab sogar ein Bild mit einem Skelett und ein weiteres, auf dem ein Galgenmännchen dargestellt war!

That's what she needed! After a few tough negotiations, Chloe obtained the 12€ from her parents and the card game was now in her possession. Once back home, Chloe locked herself away in her bedroom and unwrapped the pack of cards. They weren't just ordinary cards – far from it, each one had a different image and a roman numeral on it. This was not a problem for Chloe, who knew how to count up to at least twenty-nine in Roman numerals. A small guidebook was included with the cards. It wasn't as simple as that, though. Chloe had to learn the significance of the images. There were all sorts of them – a sun, a star, a moon, and there was even one with a skeleton, and another that resembled a hangman!

Als Chloe alle Karten studierte, entdeckte sie, dass die Art und Weise, wie die Karten gelegt wurden mussten, die Zukunft vorhersagte. Als sie dachte, dass sie genug gelernt hatte, entschied sie sich einen Test zu machen. Sie vertauschte also die Position des Messers und der Gabel auf dem Platz ihres Vaters. Sie würde also gespannt warten, wie am Abend ihre Eltern darauf reagieren. Sie legte die Glückskarten sorgfältig in Form eines Kreuzes auf, drehte sie um und analysierte dann jede Einzelne von ihnen gründlich. Es gab keine Zweifel – die Karten sagten eine Reihe von Ereignissen vorher. Ihr Vater würde das falsche Besteck zum Essen auswählen. Also beeilte sie sich am Abend den Tisch zu decken und setzte sich, noch ehe das Essen serviert war.

It was when Chloe was studying all the cards that she discovered it was the manner in which the cards were played that predicted the future. When she felt she had learned enough, she decided to do a test. One night, she decided she was going to change the place of her father's knife and fork, then see what her parents said. She carefully placed the fortune cards into a cross, turned them over, and then analyzed each of them thoroughly and how they were placed. There was no doubt – the cards were very clear in predicting the series of events. Her father would choose the wrong piece of cutlery for eating. Thus, tonight she hurried to set the table, and sat before the meal was even served.

„Na guck mal an, wir würden uns freuen, wenn du öfter mal so früh kommen würdest", witzelte ihre Mutter.

"Well, well, we like to see you come early like this more often!" said her mother jokingly.

Nach ein paar Minuten kam der Moment auf den sie gewartet hatte. Alle nahmen Platz und das Essen wurde serviert. Sie sah ihren Vater aufmerksam an und Chloe wurde ungeduldig. Los, nimm schon dein Besteck Papa, mach! Dachte Chloe, die nicht länger warten konnte. Obwohl ihr Vater geschockt von dem Verhalten seiner Tochter war, streckte er seine Hand aus. Ein wenig mehr und dann! Ohne es zu bemerken, hielt er anstatt der Gabel das Messer in der Hand.

After a few minutes, the moment she had been waiting for arrived. Everyone took their seats and the meal was served. Watching her father carefully, Chloe was growing impatient. Come on, come on, pick up your cutlery dad, go on! thought Chloe, who could not wait any longer. Although shocked by the behavior of his daughter, her father reached out his hand. A little more, and, at last! Without realizing it, he held the knife rather than the fork.

„Heureka!", rief Chloe, „es funktioniert. Die Karten hatten recht, du hast das falsche Besteck genommen!"

"Eureka!" shouted Chloe, "It works! The cards were right, you picked the wrong piece of cutlery!"

Chloe hatte endlich die Lösung für ihre Probleme gefunden. Sie probierte es viele Male aus, und die Karten sagten die Zukunft mit tadelloser Genauigkeit voraus. Erleichtert konnte Chloe endlich ein friedlicheres Leben führen. Das ging solange gut, bis eines Tages etwas Schreckliches passierte. Die Karten überbrachten eine schreckliche Nachricht. Chloe traute ihren Augen nicht – die Karten sagten vorher, dass sie die Klasse wiederholen musste.

Chloe had finally found a solution to her problems. She tried it many times, and without fail, the cards predicted the future with impeccable accuracy. Relieved, Chloe could finally live a more peaceful life. That lasted a little while until, one day, something terrible happened. The cards delivered a horrifying message. Chloe could not believe her eyes – the cards predicted that she would have to retake a grade!

Chloe legte die Karten immer und immer wieder, aber es kam jedes Mal dieselbe Kartenkombination heraus. Panisch zerriss Chloe die Karten. Das war unmöglich! Sie hatte überall Erfolg

– sie konnte die Klasse nicht wiederholen! Am nächsten Tag wurde jedoch die Vorhersage der Karten bestätigt. Als sie im Sportunterricht rannte, löste sich einer ihrer Schuhbänder. Sie musste anhalten, um sie neu zu binden und verlor viel Zeit. Chloe, die immer erste war, war dieses Mal die Letzte. Noch am selben Tag vergaß sie mehrere Wörter im Diktat, etwas, das ihr noch nie passiert war!

Intrigued initially, Chloe started over many times, but the same verdict came about several times. Panic-stricken, Chloe tore up the cards. It was impossible! She succeeded at everything – she could not retake a grade! The very next day, however, the prediction the cards made was confirmed. In sports, while she was running, one of her laces came undone. She had to stop to tie it, and she lost a lot of time. Chloe, who always came in first, almost came in last. That very same day, she forgot several words in her memory writing, something that never happened to her!

Sie hatte selbst gesagt, dass die Karten immer die Wahrheit vorhersagten, das war offensichtlich und sie musste die Klasse wohl wirklich wiederholen. Da sie wusste, was ihr bevorstand, hörte sie auf fleißig zu sein. Ihr Schicksal war vorherbestimmt und sie war nicht diejenige, die das so entschieden hatte. Sie erhielt weiterhin schlechte Noten und ihre Eltern machten sich Sorgen. Wie konnte ihre Tochter, die so klug war, so schlecht werden? Chloe konnte an nichts anderes mehr denken. Gerade als alle Hoffnung verloren schien, entschied sie sich härter an sich zu arbeiten. Ich werde das nicht zulassen, sagte sie zu sich selbst. Langsam, aber sicher arbeitete sie sich wieder hoch. Das Schuljahr kam zum Ende und Chloe hatte Angst, dass sie es nicht schaffen würde, das aufzuholen, was sie verpasst hatte.

She told herself that the cards never lied, that was obvious, and that she was going to retake her grade. Knowing the result, she stopped working. Her destiny was certain, and she wasn't the one who had decided it. She continued to get bad grades, and her parents were worried. How could their daughter, who was so smart, collapse like this? Chloe could not stop thinking about it. Just as all hope seemed to be lost, and refusing defeat, she began working harder. I will not let this defeat me! she said to herself. Slowly, but surely, she climbed back up. The end of the year arrived and Chloe was scared that she would not be able to make up what she had lost.

Endlich war es der letzte Schultag. Zitternd vor Angst wartete Chloe auf ihre Ergebnisse. Würde sie die Klasse wiederholen müssen oder würde sie in die nächste Klassenstufe kommen? Eine weitere Person war vor ihr dran und dann war sie an der Reihe. Chloe hatte gerade ihre Noten erfahren. Geschrieben mit rotem Stift stand auf dem Blatt: «Bestanden mit höchster Auszeichnung!» Chloe jubelte vor Freude. Eine Sorge weniger.

The final day had arrived. Trembling with fear, Chloe awaited her results. Would she have to retake the grade or would she move on to the next grade? One more person and then it was her turn. That was it! Chloe had just received the marks of her evaluations. Written in red pen beneath was written: "Pass with highest honours!" Chloe shouted with joy! That was one less.

Ein paar Monate später, am ersten Schultag des neuen Schuljahres, erinnerte sich Chloe an all das Geschehene vom letzten Jahr. Egal ob es eine Schicksalsfügung gab oder nicht, was zählte, war nicht das Endziel, sondern der Weg, der dorthin führte. Es passiert alles im hier und jetzt. Letztendlich, sagte sie sich, ist die Zukunft nicht geschrieben, sie wird gelebt!

A few months later, on the first day back at school, Chloe could not stop herself from thinking about all of the stories. Whether there is a destiny or not, what counts is not the final destination, but the path taken towards it. That is where everything happens. Finally, she told herself, the future isn't written, it is lived!

Geschichte 5: Leo & Basil, Der Gnom

Story 5: Leo & Basil The Gnome

Leo war ein kleiner Junge, der noch nie viel Glück gehabt hatte. Er lebte in einem kleinen Dorf auf dem Land, in einem kleinen Haus und dazu noch war er der kleinste Junge in seiner Klasse. Leo's Familie war arm und sein einziger Freund war sein Hund Michi.

Leo was a little boy who had never really had a lot of luck. He lived in a small village in the country, in a very small house and, what's more, he was the smallest boy in his grade. Leo's family was humble and his only friend was his dog, Michi.

Oft gingen Leo und Michi den ganzen Nachmittag in den Wald spazieren. Seine Klassenkameraden, die ihn nicht so

mochten, verbrachten ihre Zeit vor dem Computer oder spielten Videospiele. Seine Klassenkameraden waren nicht sehr nett zu ihm, denn sein Haus war sehr klein und er hatte kein Taschengeld, um Süßigkeiten im Dorfladen zu kaufen. Leo mochte sowieso keine Süßigkeiten. Dennoch hatte er genug davon in einem kleinen Haus zu wohnen.

Often times, Leo and Michi went walking in the woods for an entire afternoon. His schoolmates, who didn't like him very much, spent this time in front of computer screens or playing video games. His schoolmates were not very friendly to him because his house was very small and he had no pocket money to buy candy from the shop in the village. Leo did not like candy, anyway. It's true, though, that he had had enough of living in a small house.

In der Schule wollte niemand neben ihm sitzen. Leo war kein schlechter Schüler, aber er war auch nicht der Schlauste in der Klasse. Der klügste Junge in seiner Klasse war Benoit Alphonse. Sein Vater war Zahnarzt und seine Mutter Tierärztin. Sie waren reich und hatten ein riesiges Haus. Benoit war auf jeden Fall der Gemeinste von all seinen Klassenkameraden. Morgens stieg er aus dem Cabrio seines Vaters und das erste was er tat, war, Leo's Rucksack zu nehmen und alle seine Dinge auf den Boden fallen zu lassen.

At school, nobody wanted to sit next to him. Leo was not a bad student, and neither was he the brain of the class. The brightest boy in his class was Benoit Alphonse. His father was a dentist and his mother was a vet. They were rich and had an enormous house. Benoit was certainly the meanest out of all of his classmates. In the morning he got out of his father's convertible and the first thing he did was remove Leo's backpack and all his belongings fell on the ground.

Eines Tages entschied Leo, dass er alleine in den Wald gehen würde. Leo hatte eine Idee, ein großes Projekt. Er wollte eine riesige Hütte bauen, so groß, dass seine gesamte Klasse dort hineinpasste, ohne, dass jemand zerquetschen würde. Er fertigte sogar eine Planzeichnung für sein zukünftiges Haus an, das er „Villa Leo" nennen würde!

One day, Leo decided he would go to the forest alone this time. Leo had an idea in his head, a big project. He wanted to construct a huge cabin, so big that his class could get in there without being squashed. He even drew up an entire plan for his future house, which he would call Villa Leo!

Er fing an, indem er alle Zweige sammelte, die er brauchte. Er legte die Zweige auf einen Haufen und dann sammelte er viele Blätter für das Dach. Er musste ein paar Stellen frei lassen für die Fenster und am wichtigsten war der Bau einer riesigen Tür, welche sofort den Eindruck vermitteln sollte, dass dies ein sehr großes Haus war.

He started by gathering all the branches that he needed, made many piles, and then gathered a lot of leaves for the roof. He had to leave a few spaces free for the windows and, most importantly, to construct a colossal door to give the immediate impression that one was in a very large home.

Sobald er fertig mit der Arbeit war, verkündete Leo seinen Freunden, dass er ein neues Haus hatte. Sie glaubten ihm zuerst nicht, aber Leo konnte sie überzeugen und sie würden ihn am nächsten Nachmittag besuchen kommen. Am nächsten Tag fand er zu seiner Überraschung und Enttäuschung die Hütte in sich zusammengefallen vor. Das Dach war über dem Rest der Hütte zusammengesackt. In dem Moment kamen seine Schulkameraden. Sie ließen sich die Gelegenheit nicht entgehen und machten sich lustig über ihn. Traurig ging Leo zurück nach Hause. Sein Hund Michi, der ihn gut kannte, lief zu ihm, um ihn zu trösten. Aber das war nicht genug Trost für Leo.

Once he finished the work, Leo announced to his friends that he had a new house. They did not believe him at first, but Leo was successful in convincing them, and they would to go to visit the next afternoon. The very next day, to his surprise and disappointment, he found that the cabin had completely collapsed. The roof was sagging badly on the rest of the cabin. At that very moment, his schoolmates arrived. They did not miss the opportunity to mock him for it. Sad, Leo went back to his home. His dog, Michi, who knew him well, approached him to give some affection. But this wasn't enough to comfort Leo.

Ein paar Tage vergingen und Leo entschied sich, sich nicht unterkriegen zu lassen. Er zeichnete neue Pläne für seine Hütte, nahm ein paar Werkzeuge von seinem Vater mit und ging wieder in den Wald. Einen ganzen Nachmittag arbeitete er mit großen Mut an dem Bau seiner großen Hütte. Aber es war vergebens. Dieses Mal brach das Haus in dem Moment zusammen, als er den letzten Zweig anlegen wollte. Mit Tränen in den Augen setzte sich Leo auf einen Baumstumpf und vergrub den Kopf in seinen Armen. Gerade als alle Hoffnung verloren schien, passierte etwas, dass Leo nicht mehr traurig machen würde. Jemand zog leicht an seiner Jacke.

A few days passed and Leo finally decided not to let it bring him down. Drawing up new plans for his cabin, he took a few tools from his father and went into the forest again. For an entire afternoon, he worked with great courage on the reconstruction of his superb cabin. But, to no avail. This time, his house collapsed the very moment he set down the last branch. With tears in his eyes, Leo sat down on a tree stump, with his head buried in his arms. Just as all hope seemed lost, something brought Leo out of his sadness. Someone was pulling lightly on his coat.

„Hey? Kleiner Mann?"

"Hey? Mr. Little Boy?"

Leo hob seinen Kopf und zuckte vor Überraschung zusammen. Eine kleine Person, nicht größer als ein Schuh, schaute ihn an.

Leo lifted his head and jumped in surprise. A small person, no bigger than a shoe, was looking at him.

„Was ist passiert kleiner Mann? Warum bist du so traurig?"

"What happened Mr. Little Boy? Why are you so sad?"

Überrascht das jemand kleiner als er sein konnte, trocknete Leo seine Tränen und antwortete:

Surprised that someone could be smaller than him, Leo dried his tears and responded.

„Ich bin klein, ich habe kein Taschengeld, mein Haus ist sehr klein und dazu habe ich keine Freunde. Ich möchte gerne eine tolle Hütte bauen, aber ich kann nicht."

"I am small, I do not have any pocket money, my house is very small, and on top of that, I don't have any friends. I wanted to build a superb cabin, but I can't."

„Ich verstehe", sagte die kleine Person. „Und wie heißt du?"

"I see," said the small person. "And what is your name?"

„Ich heiße Leo und du, wer bist du und warum bist du so klein?"

"My name is Leo, and you, who are you, and why are you so small?"

„Ich bin Basil, der Gnom! ", sagte die kleine Person vergnügt. „Gnome sind immer klein."

"Me, I am Basil the Gnome!" said the small person gleefully. "Gnomes are always small."

„Was ist ein Gnom?", fragte Leo.

"What is a gnome?" responded Leo.

„Ein Gnom ist ein magisches Wesen aus dem Wald. Wir haben den ganzen Wald errichtet!"

"A gnome is a magical being in the forest. It is we who construct the entire forest!"

„Wow! Das ist unglaublich!", rief Leo. „Kannst du mir helfen, meine Hütte zu bauen?"

"Wow! That's incredible!" exclaimed Leo. "So you can help me build my cabin?"

„Ah, ja! Warum nicht, ich habe gerade meine Arbeit beendet. Also los! "

"Ah, yes! Why not, I just finished doing my work. Let's go!"

Leo traute seinen Augen nicht. Er hatte ein magisches Wesen getroffen und noch mehr, er hatte einen neuen Freund! Leo

und Basil, der Gnom gingen gleich an die Arbeit. Basil wusste viel über Bäume. Gut kombiniert hatten die Bäume magische Kräfte. Ein paar Eichen hier, ein paar Silberbirken da, ein paar Zedern, ein paar Haselnussbaumzweige, Lavendel für den Geruch, eine Knoblauchzehe, um die bösen Geister zu vertreiben und ein paar Zitronenbaumblätter, die laut Basil Freude bringen und alle Dinge vertreiben, die Menschen traurig machen. Als der Bau der Hütte abgeschlossen war, rief Basil ein paar seiner Freunde zu sich.

Leo could not believe his eyes. He had met a magical being and, what's more, he now had a new friend! Leo and Basil the Gnome went straight to work. Basil knew plenty of things about the trees. Mixed well, the different trees had magical powers. Some oak here, some silver birch there, a bit of cedar, a few hazel tree branches, lavender for a nice scent, a clove of garlic to get rid of the evil spirits, and a few lime tree leaves which, according to Basil, brought joy and got rid of all things that made people sad! Once the construction was complete, Basil called over a few of his friends.

„Meine Freunde werden das Haus jetzt verzaubern!", sagte Basil.

"My friends will now enchant the house!" said Basil.

Eine Fee, ein Flussgnom sowie ein gelber und schwarzer Salamander kamen, um Leo zu helfen. Sie waren alle so klein wie Basil und sehr nett. Die Fee verstreute ein wenig goldenes Puder, der Flussgnom verbreitete ein paar magische Regentropfen und der Salamander spuckte ein paar Zauberfunken.

A fairy, a river gnome, and a yellow and black salamander came to meet Leo. They were all small like Basil and very nice. The fairy scattered a little golden powder, the river gnome sprinkled some magical rain drops, and the salamander spat a few enchanted sparks.

„Das war's", sagte Basil der Gnom, „wir sind fertig". Jetzt kannst du deine Klassenkameraden in dein neues Zuhause einladen!"

"And there it is!" said Basil the Gnome, "the job is done. You can now invite your schoolmates to your new home!"

Am nächsten Tag verteilte Leo erneut Einladungen an seine Schulkameraden, die sein neues Zuhause bestaunen sollten. Wie zuvor machten sich seine Schulkameraden über ihn lustig. Aber dieses Mal wusste Leo, dass er derjenige war, der Recht behalten sollte. Sie kamen an der Hütte an, die von außen sehr klein aussah. Seine Schulkameraden kicherten aber traten dennoch ein und verfielen dem Zauber. Das Innere der Hütte war gigantisch. Es war wunderbar – es gab überall Licht, mehrere geräumige Stockwerke, Blumen und dazu waren alle seine Zauberfreunde aus dem Wald da!

The next day, Leo passed around a new invitation to visit his home. Like before, his schoolmates mocked him. But this time, Leo knew that he would be the one to win. They arrived in front of the cabin, which looked, from the outside, very small. His schoolmates sniggered but entered nonetheless, and fell under the spell. The interior of the cabin was gigantic. It was magnificent – there was light everywhere, several spacious levels, flowers, and, on top of that, all of his magical friends from the forest were there!

Und so wurden alle aus der Klasse zu Leo's besten Freunden. Michi würde jedoch immer sein bester Freund sein, das war sicher. Und seit dem Tag kam die Klasse am Wochenende, anstatt Computer oder Videospiele zu spielen, viel lieber in die „Villa Leo" im Wald.

Thus, the entire class became Leo's best friends, though Michi would always be his closest friend, for sure. And since that day, every weekend, instead of playing on the computer or playing video games, the entire class has fun at Villa Leo in the forest.

Chapter "Good Will"

Helping others without expectation of anything in return has been proven to lead to increased happiness and satisfaction in life.

We would love to give you the chance to experience that same feeling during your reading or listening experience today...

All it takes is a few moments of your time to answer one simple question:

> **Would you make a difference in the life of someone you've never met—without spending any money or seeking recognition for your good will?**

If so, we have a small request for you.

If you've found value in your reading or listening experience today, we humbly ask that you take a brief moment right now to leave an honest review of this book. It won't cost you anything but 30 seconds of your time—just a few seconds to share your thoughts with others.

Your voice can go a long way in helping someone else find the same inspiration and knowledge that you have.

Scan the QR code below:

OR

 Visit the link below:

https://geni.us/nAHr5N

Thank you in advance!

Geschichte 6: Arthur Nevus & Das Himmlische Glas

Story 6: Arthur Nevus & The Celestial Glass

Ins Weltall zu reisen und auf der Suche nach anderen Zivilisationen im Weltall zu sein ...genau das sind die verrückten Träume von Arthur Nevus! Als sehr neugieriger und eifriger Junge hatte der junge Arthur schon immer den Blick in die Sterne gerichtet und den Kopf in den Wolken. Sein Schlafzimmer ist ein echtes Labor, das den größten Gelehrten würdig ist. Hier findest du NASA Poster, ein Haufen Geräte und alle Mittel, die ein Astronaut so zur Hand haben sollte.

To travel to space, in search of other civilizations across the entire universe ... these are the crazy dreams that Arthur Nevus has! A very curious and ambitious boy, the young Arthur always has his gaze towards the stars and his head in the clouds. His bedroom is a veritable laboratory worthy of the greatest savants. You find NASA posters, a pile of gadgets, and all the tools an astronaut should have on hand.

Jeden Abend suchte Arthur mit seinem Teleskop durch sein Dachfenster das Weltall ab. Leider kam es am vergangenen Wochenende, während er ein kompliziertes Experiment durchführte, zu einer verhängnisvollen Katastrophe, die sein Teleskop komplett zerstörte! Zum Glück bekam er an seinem Geburtstag ein wenig Geld für ein neues Teleskop. Alles war vorbereitet. Am Mittwoch Nachmittag hatte er eine Verabredung im Weltallladen an der Ecke der Straße.

Every evening, Arthur searched outer space with his telescope through his skylight. Unfortunately, last weekend while he was carrying out a complicated experiment, a disastrous catastrophe completely destroying his telescope! Luckily, he was given a small amount of money to buy a new telescope on his birthday. Everything was set. On Wednesday afternoon he had an appointment at the space store at the corner of the road.

Als Arthur in den Laden trat, fühlte er sich, als wenn er in einem Raumschiff wäre. Es gab Astronautenanzüge in verschiedenen Ausführungen, Modell-Raketenschiffe, Miniatur Repliken aller Planeten, Teleskope und viele andere Dinge, die Arthur gerne kaufen würde. Während er durch die Gänge wanderte, erschien eine lustig aussehende Person zwischen zwei der Regalen. Er sprach mit einem Kauderwelsch, den Arthur Nevus überhaupt nicht verstand.

As Arthur entered the store, he felt as if he had been transported in a space vessel. There were astronaut suits of several varieties, model rocket ships, miniature replicas of all the planets, telescopes, and lots of other things that Arthur would have liked to buy. While he was wandering through the aisles, a funny looking person appeared between two of the shelves. He spoke a kind of gibberish that Arthur Nevus did not understand at all.

„Hallo kleiner Mann, was ich kann ich für dich tun?"

"Well good day little man, what can I do for you?"

Er hatte einen kleinen Büschel unordentlicher weißer Haare und eine große Brille, die seine großen Augen wulstig erscheinen ließ. Das muss ein großer Gelehrter sein, dachte Arthur.

He had a small tuft of messy white hair and a large pair of glasses that made his large eyes bulge. This has to be a great savant, thought Arthur.

„Hallo, ich würde gerne ein neues Teleskop kaufen", sagte er .

"Hello sir, I would like to buy a new telescope," he responded.

„Es tut mir leid, ich habe keine Teleskope zu verkaufen, junger Mann."

"I am sorry, I do not have any more telescopes to sell, my young gentleman."

„Oh, aber das haben Sie doch!", rief Arthur. „Ich habe viele am Eingang gesehen."

"Oh, but you do!" shouted Arthur. "I saw plenty in the entrance."

„Das sind nur Spielzeuge für die Dekoration. Los, mach das du rauskommst, ich muss arbeiten!"

"Those are nothing but poor toys used for decoration. Go, go, on your way, I must work!"

Aber Arthur war noch nicht fertig. Nach langen Verhandlungen war er endlich erfolgreich und der Gelehrte hörte ihm zu.

But Arthur had not said his final word. After some long negotiations, he was finally successful in obtaining something from the savant.

„Hör zu junger Mann, ich würde dir gerne helfen, aber du musst mir etwas versprechen."

"Listen my little man, I would like to help you, but you have to promise me something."

„Okay!", bestätigte Arthur.

"Okay!" confirmed Arthur.

„Ich werde dir das letzte Teleskop leihen, das ich habe, das ist das einzige, was ich nie verkauft habe und auch nie verkaufen werde!"

"I will lend you the last telescope that I have, the only one that I have never sold and will never sell!"

„Warum?" fragte Arthur.

"Why?" asked Arthur.

„Weil es nicht mir gehört natürlich!"

"Because it does not belong to me, of course!"

„Warum gehört es dir nicht?"

"Who does it belong to?"

„Das ist ein Geheimnis ... aber ich möchte, dass du mir versprichst, dass du es mir in gutem Zustand zurückgibst! Ist das klar?"

"That is a secret ... but, I want you to promise me that you will return it to me in perfect condition! Is that clear?"

„Ganz klar!"

"Perfectly clear, sir!"

Der Mann kam mit einem lustig aussehenden Gerät zurück, das nicht so aussah wie die anderen. Arthur konnte nicht glauben, dass dieses Ding ins Weltall blicken konnte. Ein Bürostuhl war

mit einem riesigen Fahrradrad mit Schnüren verbunden. Die Pedalen lagen auf den Armlehnen und auf der Oberseite befand sich eine große Glühbirne.

The savant came back with a funny looking machine unlike all the others. Arthur did not believe that thing could see into space. An office seat was connected to a huge bike wheel with strings. The pedals were placed on the armrests and on the top of it there was a large bulb.

„Sag jetzt bitte nichts. Du wirst sehen, dass es funktioniert. Das ist himmlisches Glas!"

"No commentary please. You will see, it works. This is the Celestial Glass!"

Ehe Artur ging, gab ihm der Mann eine große Brille, wie er sie selber trug.

Before Arthur left, the savant gave him a pair of large glasses like his own.

„Vergiss nicht die Brille aufzusetzen, sonst wirst du nichts sehen! Los! Gute Reise mein lieber Arthur Nevus. "

"Don't forget to put them on, otherwise you will not be able to see anything! Go! Happy travels, my dear Arthur Nevus."

Dann kam die Nacht und Arthur setzte sich auf den Sitz des Fahrrads. Als er zu treten begann, drehte sich das Rad und die Glühbirne erhellte. Plötzlich und total überraschend fühlte Arthur, wie er in Richtung Himmel flog! Voller Panik kniff er die Augen fest zusammen. Nach ein paar Momenten beruhigten sich die Turbulenzen und Arthur öffnete seine Augen wieder. Was er sah, war unglaublich! Er war direkt in einer riesigen Stadt, wo viele Autos über dem Boden flogen und gigantische Raumschiffe über Wolkenkratzer glitten.

At long last, nightfall came and Arthur planted himself into the seat of the machine. As he began pedaling, the wheel began to turn and the bulb lit up. All of a sudden and quite unexpectedly, Arthur felt himself being propelled towards the sky! Panic-filled, he closed his eyes tightly. After a few moments, the turbulence calmed and Arthur reopened his eyes. What he saw was incredible! He was face-to-face with a huge town where lots of cars flew above the ground and gigantic vessels glided over skyscrapers.

Während er auf die wunderbare Landschaft schaute, kam ein kleiner Junge, der im selben Alter wie er war.

While he was gazing at this amazing landscape, a young boy, about the same age as him, arrived.

„Oh hallo! Bist du mit Professor Rumerec hier?"

"Oh, hello! Have you come here with professor Rumerec?!"

„Ähm, ich kenne keinen Professor Rumerec!", antwortete Arthur.

"Um, I do not know a professor Rumerec! Arthur replied.

„Natürlich kennst du ihn – ich bin derjenige, der ihm dieses Gerät gegeben hat!"

"But of course you do — I'm the one who gave him this machine!"

„Ah! Der verrückte Wissenschaftler in dem Weltallladen! Also wer bist du, dass du weißt, wie man so ein Gerät baut und wo sind wir hier?"

"Ah! The crazy scientist in the space store! Well, who are you to know how to build a machine like that, and where are we?"

„Mein Name ist Annko Velarenne! Wir sind hier auf dem Planeten Zalka, genauer gesagt auf der anderen Seite des Universums!"

"My name is Annko Velarenne! We are on the planet Zalka, precisely on the other side of the universe!"

Annko erzählte Arthur die Geschichte ihrer Zivilisation – die Kolonisierung der Galaxie, die Entdeckung des Universums und viele andere Dinge. Dann erzählte er Arthur schreckliche Neuigkeiten. Der Planet Zalka war in sehr schlechtem Zustand. Die Industrie auf ihrem Planeten hat die ganze Atmosphäre zerstört, die Ozeane und Luft verschmutzt und die Wälder verbrannt. Der junge Annko Velarenne war sehr traurig, weil sie ihren Planeten verlassen mussten und lange Zeit in seinem Raumschiff leben würden, ehe sie ein anderes Zuhause finden würden.

Annko shared with Arthur the story of their civilization — the colonization of the galaxy, the exploration of the Universe, and many other things. Then, he told Arthur some terrible news. The planet Zalka was in very bad shape. The industry on their planet had destroyed the entire atmosphere, dirtied the oceans, polluted the air, and burned down the forests. The young Annko Velarenne was very sad because they were going to leave their planet and live for a long time in his vessel before finding another home.

„Aber wie ist das möglich? Habt ihr keine Lösung gefunden?", **fragte Arthur.**

"But, how is that possible? Haven't you found a solution?" asked Arthur.

„Ja, aber es ist zu spät ... wir können die Zeit nicht zurückdrehen."

"Yes, but it is too late ... we can't go back in time."

Arthur und Annko redeten viele Stunden. Aber Annko musste dann zu seinen Eltern, und mit seinem Raumschiff abfahren. Es war Zeit für die Einwohner von Zalka ihren Planeten zu verlassen. Arthur tat Annko sehr Leid. Nachdem der Junge weg war, ging Arthur zurück zum Gerät des Gelehrten. Er wachte am nächsten Morgen in seinem Bett auf, das himmlische Glas zeigte in Richtung seines Dachfensters.

Arthur and Annko discussed this for many hours. But Annko had to rejoin his parents to leave in their space vessel. It was time for the residents of Zalka to leave their planet. Arthur was very sad for Annko too. When he had left, Arthur returned to the savant's machine. He woke up the next morning in his bed, the Celestial Glass turned towards his skylight.

Er kam gerade von dem verrücktesten Erlebnis aller Zeiten zurück. Jetzt wusste er, dass es noch andere Menschen im Weltall gab, die sie beobachteten. Arthur ging, um das himmlische Glas dem verrückten Gelehrten, dem bekannten Professor Rumerec zurückzugeben. Und in dem Moment dachte er an die Tatsache, dass wir alle sehr glücklich sein

konnten, auf unserem Planeten zu leben. Es gab immer noch Bäume, Ozeane und Luft zum Atmen! Ich werde dem Gelehrten alles erzählen, denn das, was auf dem Planeten Zalka passiert ist, darf auf keinen Fall bei uns passieren! Wenn wir ein tolles Zuhause haben, dann müssen wir auch gut darauf aufpassen. Ein paar Jahre später wurde der junge Arthur Nevus der beste Gelehrte aller Zeiten, er engagierte sich für die Rettung der Erde und war der erste Entdecker des Weltraums.

He had just come from having the craziest experience of all time. Now, he knew there were other humans in space who were watching them. Arthur went to return the Celestial Glass to the crazy savant, the famous professor Rumerec. And at that very moment, he thought about the fact that we are very lucky to live on our planet. There are still trees, oceans, and air to breathe! I will tell the president everything, what happened on the planet Zalka absolutely cannot happen to us! When we have a great home, we have to take good care of it! A few years later, the young Arthur Nevus became the best savant of all time, engaged in saving the planet earth, and the first explorer of outer space.

Geschichte 7: Nicht Gesehen, Nicht Geschehen

Story 7: Not Seen, Not Taken!

Hallo, mein Name ist Tommy. Ich bin meistens freundlich, aber ich bin nicht gut in der Schule. Zum Glück habe ich eine gute Methode gefunden, um das zu umgehen – indem ich schmmle. Ihr solltet wissen, dass Schummeln ein echtes Talent erfordert! Es gibt viele verschiedene Wege, um zu schummeln, aber das Schwerste ist, sich nicht erwischen zu lassen. Wenn Tests geschrieben werden, brauchst du nur ein Spickzettel im Federmäppchen zu haben, das war's schon. Was? Du weißt nicht, was ein Spickzettel ist? Dann wird es Zeit für eine Lektion, mein Freund! Ein Spickzettel ist ein kleines Stück Papier, auf dem man Dinge schreibt, die man am Tag der Prüfung nicht vergessen darf. Spickzettel funktionieren gut, aber das Problem ist, dass sie schwierig zu verstecken sind. Denn nach einer gewissen Zeit fällt es auf, wenn man ständig in das Federmäppchen starrt.

Hello, my name is Tommy. I am mostly friendly, but I am not very good at school. Luckily, I have found a fool-proof method for getting by — I cheat! You must understand, cheating requires a certain talent! There are many different ways to cheat, but the hardest part is not getting caught. For writing tests, all you need is a cheat-sheet in your pencil case and there you have it. What?! You don't know what a cheat-sheet is? It's time to give you a lesson, my friends! A cheat-sheet is a small piece of paper, on which you write things you don't want to forget on the day of the exam. It works well as a technique, but the problem is that it is difficult to hide. After a while, it becomes obvious when you're looking in your pencil case all the time.

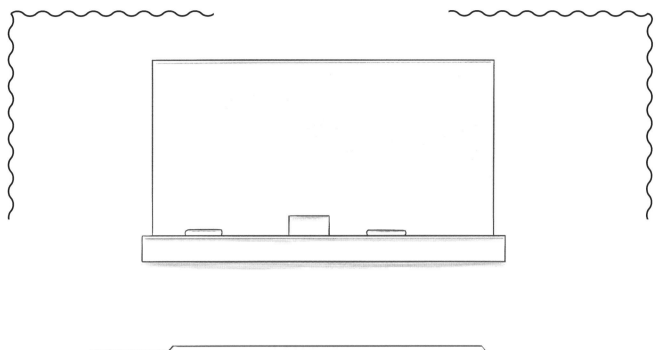

Am meisten gefällt mir die Armtechnik. Einmal habe ich die Hälfte der Antworten für den Test auf meinen linken Arm geschrieben und die andere Hälfte auf den anderen Arm. Macht das aber nicht im Sommer, denn wenn ihr wegen der Hitze euren Pullover auszieht, wird jeder sehen, dass ihr geschummelt habt. Der Schlüssel für den Erfolg hierbei ist, den Spickzettel niemanden zeigen, nicht mal deinen Freunden. Die petzen dann, bestimmt kennst du das! Also sage niemandem, was du machst. Und ja, ich sollte sagen, dass dies besondere Kompetenz erfordert und viele Jahre Übung. Ich persönlich begann mit dem Schummeln, als ich noch sehr jung war. Bereits in der Vorschule testete ich meine vielversprechenden Fähigkeiten aus.

I really like the arm technique. One time, I wrote half of the answers for my test on the left arm, and the other half on the right arm. However, don't do it in the summer, because if you take off your pullover due to the heat, everyone will see that you have cheated. The key to being successful at this is to never be exposed, even by your friends. The tattle-tales, you know them! So, mum's the word, don't tell anyone what you're up to. And yes, I should just say that this requires unusual expertise and many years of training. Personally, I started cheating when I was very young. Already in the youngest section of pre-school, I was testing my promising skills.

Sofort zu Beginn des Schuljahres in der ersten Klasse, wusste ich, dass es meine Bestimmung war. Instinktiv ohne darüber nachzudenken, schaute ich über die Schulter meines Nachbarn, um bei ihm abzuschreiben. Eines Tages stahl ich sogar ein goldenes Sternchen von Christelle, die hinter mir saß, damit ich schneller eine Karte bekam. Ich weiß nicht, ob es an eurer Schule auch so ist, aber an meiner Schule bekommt man, eine Karte, wenn man zehn goldene Sterne hat. Und wenn man zehn Karten hat, bekommt man ein tolles Poster! Ich musste natürlich schummeln, um meine zehn Karten zu erhalten. Das habe ich erfolgreich getan und die Bezahlung war ein wunderbares Poster von Harry Potter. Von dem Tag an sagte ich mir selbst, dass das Schummeln wie eine Art Magie ist. Unter uns gesagt, wissen wir jedoch das Magie dumm ist und nicht existiert.

But it was the beginning of the school year in the first grade when I knew right away that it was my calling. Instinctively, without even thinking about it, I looked over my neighbor's shoulder to copy what he had written. One day, I even stole a gold star from Christelle, who was behind me, so as to get a card faster. I don't know if it's the same at your school, but at mine, when you have ten gold stars, you get a card. And when you have ten cards, you get an awesome poster! Without a doubt,

I had to cheat to obtain my ten cards. It is what I did successfully, and the payoff was that I got a magnificent poster of Harry Potter. From that day on, I told myself that to be a cheater is sort of like doing magic. Between you and me, we know that magic is stupid and doesn't exist.

Aber in diesem Jahr gibt es ein Problem! Ich habe einen neuen Lehrer, Herr Boniface. Ich kann dir sagen, Herr Boniface war nicht von gestern. Er ist ein alter Lehrer, der alle Tricks der Schummler kennt. Vom ersten Tag an bemerkte er mein Talent in den Fächern und behielt mich ständig im Auge. Aber das beunruhigte mich nicht. In diesem Spiel war ich der Meister. Ich musste eine Strategie entwickeln, um ihn auszutricksen. Ich ging sogar so weit, mir eine ganze Geschichte einzuprägen,

um sein Misstrauen mir gegenüber zu beseitigen! Ich kann dir versichern, dass ich lieber schummelte – es machte viel mehr Spaß. Er war also verunsichert, da er meine Machenschaften nicht entdecken konnte. Ich machte falsche Spickzettel und schrieb Buchstaben auf meine Arme. Die ganze Klasse lachte an dem Tag hysterisch. Es war Diktat-Tag. Ich rollte meine Ärmel hoch und las den Satz, der auf meine Arme geschrieben war. Herr Boniface war sehr wütend, als er bemerkte, dass ich nicht schummelte.

Except, this year there is drama! I have a new teacher, Mr. Boniface. I can tell you, Mr. Boniface was not born yesterday. He is an old teacher who knows all the tricks of cheaters. From the first day, he noticed my talents in subjects and he kept an eye on me constantly. But I would not let it faze me. At this game, I am the master. I had to develop a strategy to parry my adversary's blows. I even went as far as memorizing an entire story to erase his suspicions! I can assure you that I prefer cheating — it is much more fun. So, very gently, I sowed doubt in his mind and he could not read my games. I had made fake cheat-sheets and wrote love letters on my arms. Moreover, the entire class laughed hysterically that day. It was dictation day. I rolled up my sleeves and read the phrases that were written on my arms. Mr. Boniface was very angry when he realized that I was not cheating.

Nach vielen Schabernacken war ich erfolgreich in meinem Spiel und Herr Boniface wusste nicht mehr, wo er hingucken sollte. Danach konnte ich richtig loslegen. Und es funktionierte gut, denn in dem Jahr mussten wir eine Arbeit schreiben über ein Thema, das wir selbst auswählen konnten. Wir bildeten Dreiergruppen und wisst ihr, was ich machte? Natürlich, ich schummelte, um mit guten Personen zusammenzukommen. Antoine und Jamila waren beide gute Schülerinnen in der Klasse. Ich musste sehr lachen, als ich den Blick von Herrn Boniface sah, den er mir zuwarf. Aber es war wie gute Schummler sagen: Nichts gesehen, nichts geschehen!

After many practical jokes, I was successful in my game, and Mr. Boniface did not know which way to turn anymore. I could then start work for real. And it turned out well, because that year we had to write a paper on a subject matter chosen randomly. We formed groups of three, and do you know what I did? Of course I cheated to be paired with good people. Antoine and Jamila were the best students in class. I could not help but laugh hard as soon as I saw the accusatory look Mr. Boniface gave me. But it's like we great cheaters always say: Not seen, not taken!

Andererseits fühlte ich mich ein wenig dumm, weil ich es nicht geschafft hatte – ich war nicht erfolgreich beim Schummeln gewesen, auch wenn ich das leichteste Thema hatte. Das Glück war auf meiner Seite und das Thema, das mir und meinem netten Team gegeben wurde, war das Folgende: Magie in der Literatur und im Kino. Du wirst es nicht glauben, aber mir passierte etwas Merkwürdiges während der Arbeit, die wir in der Klasse in dem Jahr machten. Ja, ja, es stimmt. Ich entwickelte eine Leidenschaft für das Thema! So sehr, dass ich am Ende all die Nachforschungen betrieb. Ich las mindestens sechs Bücher, schaute ein Dutzend Filme, ging in den Zirkus und sogar ins Theater. Es war fabelhaft; ich lernte viele merkwürdige Dinge und dazu entdeckte ich, wie es war, aus eigener Kraft erfolgreich zu sein! Am Ende des Jahres stellten wir das Projekt in der Klasse vor und unsere Gruppe erhielt die beste Note in der Klasse! Unsere Darstellung war so gut, dass Herr Boniface es allen Klassen empfahl und sogar unseren Eltern.

On the other hand, I felt a bit stupid because I had messed up – I did not succeed in cheating when I had the easiest subject. Chance was on my side and the subject that was given to us, my fine team and me, was the following: magic in literature and in the cinema. You will not believe me, but something strange happened to me during all of the work we did in that class that year. Yes, yes, it's true, I was completely passionate about the subject! So much so that it was me who was doing all the research.

I read at least six books, watched dozens of films, I went to the circus, and even to the theatre. It was fabulous; I learned a lot of extraordinary things, and most of all, I discovered what it's like to be successful of your own accord! At the end of the year, we presented in front of the class and our group received the best mark in the class! Our exposition was so good that Mr. Boniface distributed it to all the classes, and even to the parents.

Ich war noch nie stolzer auf mich selbst und seit dem Tag habe ich aufgehört zu schummeln. Ich erkannte, dass das, was du selbst machst, viel mehr Wert hat!

I have never been as proud of myself and since that day I have stopped cheating. I realized that what you do on your own has a lot of merit!

Geschichte 8: Missa Rose im Land Cave-in-Brac

Story 8: Missa Rose in Cave-in-Brac Country

Missa Rose ist ein junges, kleines Mädchen vom Sunev-Stamm. Mit spitzen Ohren und einem dünnen Gesicht sind die Sunev die Elfen im Wald der hohen Berge. In diesem Elfenstamm erzählt eine alte Legende die Geschichte eines großen weisen Mannes, namens Sage Serhem-Hott, der eines Tages vom Gipfel des Berges mit einem magischen Stein zurückkam. Der Stein von Tipheret, auch bekannt als Sonnenstein. Während die Elfen vom Sunev-Stamm friedlich lebten, griff sie eine eifersüchtige und teuflische Bande von Kobolden aus dem dunklen Königreich von Kuhtmal an, um ihnen den Sonnenstein zu stehlen. Eines Tages wurde die Mutter von Missa Rose sehr krank. Keine Magie konnte sie von ihrer mysteriösen Krankheit heilen.

Missa Rose is a young, small girl from the Sunev Tribe. With pointy ears and a thin face, the Sunev are elves of the forest in the high mountains. In this elf tribe, an old legend tells the story of a Great Wiseman and Sage Serhem-Hott who came back one day from the summit of the mountain with a magical stone, The Stone of Tipheret, also known as the Sun Stone. While the elves in the Sunev tribe lived peacefully, a band of jealous and evil goblins of the dark kingdom of Kuhtmal attacked them to steal the Sun Stone. One day, Missa Rose's mom fell terribly ill. Not a single magical thing cured her of this mysterious illness.

Missa Rose entschied sich den großen Weisen Sehrhem Hott aufzusuchen, der weit oben nah am Gipfel wohnte. Er sagte, dass es nötig wäre, eine größere magische Kraft zu benutzen, um ihre Mutter von dieser schrecklichen Krankheit zu heilen. Missa Rose dachte lange Zeit nach, ehe sie zu dem Schluss kam, dass der große weise Mann auf jeden Fall von dem Stein von Tipheret sprach, dem Sonnenstein. Am nächsten Tag nahm Missa ihren Stock und ein Bündel Kleider und begann ihre

Reise in das Dorf, um das furchterregende Königreich der Kobolde zu finden. Sie wusste, was sie erwartete. Man sagte, dass das Dorf von einem kinderessenden Monster, einem Wolf, einem Zauberer und stehlenden Kobolden bewohnt sei!

Missa Rose then decided to pay a visit to the Great Wiseman Serhem-Hott who lived above, closer to the top of the mountain. He judged that it was necessary to use a great magical power to save her mom from this terrible illness. Missa Rose thought for a long time before concluding that the Great Wiseman was certainly talking about the Stone of Tipheret, the Sun Stone. The next day, Missa took her stick and her bundle of clothes and began her journey into the valley to find the frightening kingdom of the goblins. She knew what was waiting for her. It had been said that the valley was inhabited by a child-eating ogre, a wolf, a sorcerer, and thieving goblins!

Nachdem sie den ganzen Tag gelaufen war, kam Missa Rose in der Stadt von Noblerock an. Es war der perfekte Ort zum Ausruhen. Hier gab es nichts außer Menschen. Sie machte sich auf den Weg in einen Gasthof, wo sich ein Junge ihr näherte. Er hatte auch die Legende des Sonnensteins gehört und wollte ihn finden. Sein Name war Iseod und sein Vater, ein Zauberer, hatte ihm einen Mondstein gegeben. Glücklich darüber, einen Verbündeten auf ihrer Reise zu treffen, akzeptierte Missa Rose Iseod's Gesellschaft.

After an entire day of walking, Missa Rose arrived in the town of Noblerock. It was the perfect place to rest. Here, there was nothing but humans. She made her way inside an inn, where a young boy approached her. By chance, he had also heard the legend of the Sun Stone, and wanted to find it. His name was Iseod, and his magician father had given him the Moon Stone. Excited to meet an ally in her quest, Missa Rose accepted Iseod joining her.

Bei Sonnenuntergang hatten Iseod mit seinem Mondstein und Missa Rose mit ihrer Elfenmagie genug Mut, um sich den Monstern im Dorf zu stellen. Sie machten keine Pause. Direkt am ersten Tag wurden sie von einer Gruppe sabbernder Kröten angegriffen. Am zweiten Tag war es eine Horde teuflischer Feen und am dritten Tag war es ein großer Drache mit drei Schwänzen! Gott sei Dank hatte Iseod ein Zauberschwert bei sich und Missa Rose hatte einen Zauberstab. Sie besiegten erfolgreich alle ihre Feinde. Aber das Schlimmste stand ihnen noch bevor. Nur wenige sind je vom dunklen Königreich von Kuhtmal lebend zurückgekommen. Am zehnten Tag kamen sie endlich an ihrem Ziel an. Auf einem großen Holzschild stand: Verflucht sei der, der das Land von Cave-in-Brac, das Königreich von Kuhtmal betritt!

At sunrise, Iseod, with his Moon Stone, and Missa Rose, with her elf magic, left with a lot of courage to confront the monsters of the valley. They weren't given a break at all. Straightaway on the first day, they were attacked by a group of slobbering toads. The second day, it was a hoard of evil fairies, and on the third day, it was a big dragon with three tails! Luckily, Iseod had an enchanted sword with him and Missa Rose had a magical wand. They were successful in eliminating all their enemies on their own. But the worst was yet to come. Almost no one had ever returned alive from the dark Kingdom of Kuhtmal. On the tenth day, they finally arrived at their destination. A big wooden sign said: Cursed be those who enter Cave-in-Brac Country, the Great Kingdom of Kuhtmal!

Es war schrecklich. Ein wenig weiter hinter dem Schild konnten sie eine große Steintreppe sehen, die in die Tiefe hinabging. Hier begann ihr wirkliches Abenteuer. Sie nahmen ihren ganzen Mut zusammen und betraten das teuflische Königreich der Kobolde. Die Treppen gingen tief hinab und kein einziges

Licht leuchtete ihnen. Aber Iseod hatte mehr als einen Trick in seiner Tasche. Ausgestattet mit seinem Mondstein und mit der Hilfe von einem sehr alten Zauberspruch, konnte er Licht in die Dunkelheit bringen. Je weiter sie kamen, umso mehr mussten sie ihre Nasen zuhalten, da der Geruch in der Luft faulig war.

It was terrifying. A bit further along, behind the sign, they could see a big stone staircase that descended into the depths of the earth. It was then that their true quest began. Taking their courage in both hands, they went into the evil kingdom of the Goblins. The stairs descended very deep and not a single light lit their way. But Iseod had more than one trick in his bag. Equipped with his Moon Stone, and with the help of a very old magical spell, he was able to disperse the darkness with light. The more they advanced, the more they were forced to hold their noses, as the smell in the air was putrid!

Plötzlich hörten sie Rufe! Das waren Kobolde, die riefen. Sie mussten wohl das Licht von Iseod's Mondstein gesehen haben.

All of a sudden, they heard shouting! It was the Goblins shouting as they must have been forewarned by the light emitted by Iseod's Moon Stone.

„Schnell!", sagten sie gleichzeitig. „Wir müssen uns verstecken!"

"Quick!" they said at the same time, "We must hide!"

Sie liefen los und versuchten eine sichere Stelle zu finden.

They ran flat out trying to find a safe spot.

„Da! Hier, hinter dem Felsen!", rief Missa Rose.

"There! Right there, behind that rock!" yelled Missa Rose.

Endlich wussten sie, warum sich ihre lange Reise gelohnt hatte. Direkt hinter ihnen, nicht weit von dem Stein, wo sie sich versteckten, führte eine Hängebrücke zu einer großen Säule und darin lag der berühmte Stein von Tipheret, der Sonnenstein. Leider schien er in der völligen Dunkelheit des Königreichs Kuhtmal nicht mehr. Iseod und Missa Rose beeilten sich, ihn zu holen, ehe die Kobolde kamen und dann versteckten sie sich wieder.

It was there that they finally saw the purpose of their mission. Just behind them, not far from the rock where they were hiding, a suspension-bridge led to a big column, and embedded in it was the famous Stone of Tipheret, the Sun Stone. Sadly, in complete darkness in the middle of the Kingdom of Kuhtmal, it did not shine anymore. Iseod and Missa Rose hurried to recover it before the Goblins arrived, then returned to hide.

Als sie sahen, dass der Sonnenstein verschwunden war, liefen die Kobolde in Richtung Säule. Iseod verließ sein Versteck und mit der Hilfe von seinem Zauberschwert schnitt er schnell die Stränge durch, die die Brücke stabil hielten. Die Kobolde konnten nicht zurück und Iseod konnte jetzt zusammen mit Missa Rose an die Oberfläche zurückkehren! Der Weg zurück schien viel einfacher als der Weg hierher. Auf dem Weg zur Menschenstadt Noblerock, bat Missa Rose Iseod sie nach Hause zu begleiten. Da er sich heimlich in Missa Rose verliebt hatte, stimmte er ohne zu zögern zu!

Seeing that the Sun Stone had disappeared, the Goblins rushed towards the column. Iseod left his hiding spot, and with the help of his enchanted sword, he violently cut the cords that held the bridge. The Goblins could not turn around and Iseod, along with Missa Rose, could now return to the surface! The route back proved to be calmer than the way in. On the path to the Human town of Noblerock, Missa Rose asked Iseod to accompany her back home. Having secretly fallen in love with Missa Rose, he accepted without hesitation!

Als sie ankamen, war Missa Rose's Mutter dem Tode nahe. Mit der Hilfe des ganzen Stammes brachten sie sie zum Haus in Serhem-Hott zum großen Weisen. Als er sie ansah, fürchtete er jedoch, dass es zu spät war, sie wieder zu heilen – der Sonnenstein wäre vielleicht nicht ausreichend stark. Nach einigen großen magischen Beschwörungen, schien der Sonnenstein sehr hell. Während die Stunden vergingen, tat der große Weise alles, was in seiner Macht stand, um Missa Rose's Mutter zu retten, aber trotzdem war ihre Krankheit stärker als seine Magie.

When they arrived, Missa Rose's mother was close to death. With the help of the entire tribe, they brought her to the house of Serhem-Hott the Great Wiseman. When he looked at her, however, he feared it was too late, that she was too ill — the Sun Stone would perhaps not suffice. After some great magical invocations, the Sun Stone shone very brightly. During the hours that passed, the Great Wiseman did everything in his power to save Missa Rose's mother, but in spite of this, her illness was stronger than he was.

Als ihre Mutter ihren letzten Atemzug tat und ihr Leben in andere Sphären verschwinden wollte, umarmte Missa Rosa ihre Mutter ganz fest und sagte „Ich liebe dich, Mama, geh nicht!" Alle blieben still und wussten nicht, was jetzt passieren würde, aber plötzlich verließ die Krankheit ihren Körper! Missa Rose's Mutter erholte sich und konnte ihrer Tochter antworten, „Ich liebe dich auch mein Schatz." „Hurra!", rief der Stamm freudig – sie hatten die Krankheit geheilt! Später, nach all ihren Abenteuern heirateten Missa Rose und Iseod. Sie vereinten die Menschen und die Elfenstämme und wurden nie wieder von Kobolden angegriffen!

As her mother was about to take her last breath, and her life was about to depart for other horizons, Missa Rose hugged her mother very, very hard, saying, "I love you mom, don't go!" Everyone stayed quiet, not knowing what was going to happen then, all of a sudden, the illness left her! Missa Rose's mother recovered and could then respond to her daughter, "I love you too my dear." "Hooray!" the tribe shouted for joy — they had cured the illness! Later on, Missa Rose and Iseod, after all their adventures, finally got married. They unified the human and elf tribes and they were never attacked by the Goblins again!

Als die Zeit für Missa Rose gekommen war, um selbst Mutter zu werden, sagte sie: „Am Ende ist Liebe, wie immer die beste Art von Magie!"

Here is what Missa Rose said as soon as the time came for her to become a mother: "Finally, love, like always, will remain the best kind of magic!"

Geschichte 9: Mateo Teilt Nichts

Story 9: Mateo Shares Nothing

Mateo lebt auf einem riesigen Privatgrundstück im Herzen des Waldes. Sein Zuhause ist eine kleine Burg und der Garten ist voll mit unzähligen Spielzeugen. Was er besitzt, würde wohl jeden eifersüchtig machen! Er hat ein Trampolin, einen Pool, eine Riesenrutsche, ein kleines elektrisches Fahrrad, Minigolf und viele anderen Dinge, die jedes Kind weltweit glücklich machen würden. Mateo geht immer gut gekleidet in die Schule mit Keksen und Kuchen für die Pause und natürlich einer vollen Tasche mit Süßigkeiten! Mateo hatte immer alles: Murmeln, Dragon Ball Z Karten, seltene Pokemon Karten und jede Art von Videospiel-Konsole mit allen Spielen, die es gab. Man kann sagen, es fehlt ihm an nichts.

Mateo lives in a huge private property in the heart of the forest. His house resembles a small castle and his garden is filled with an uncountable number of toys. What he has would render anyone jealous! He has a trampoline, a pool, a giant slide, a small electric bike, mini-golf, and many other things that would please any kid in the world. Mateo always goes to school well dressed, with cookies and cake for recess, and, of course, a full bag of candy! In any case, Mateo always has everything; marbles, Dragon Ball Z cards, rare Pokemon cards, and every video game console with every game. One might say that he's not short of anything.

Mateo's größtes Problem ist es, auch wenn er alles hat, dass er nie etwas teilen möchte. Selbst wenn er in der Cafeteria etwas nicht aufisst, teilt er die Reste nicht. Er scheint nicht gemein, aber niemand versteht, warum er so egoistisch ist – er möchte alles für sich alleine und nur für sich. Und deswegen hatte Mateo auch keine Freunde. Niemand wollte mit ihm spielen, weil er immer überall der Beste sein wollte. Deshalb saß Mateo immer alleine auf der Bank in der Pause. Er sitzt dort mit seinem Handy, seinen Süßigkeiten und seinen Keksen. Weder die Mädchen noch die Jungen wollen mit ihm sprechen. Obwohl Mateo alles hat, ist ihm schrecklich langweilig. Als einziges Kind hat er keine Geschwister, mit denen er am Wochenende Spaß haben könnte. Und wenn er durch die Stadt läuft, um

In fact, Mateo's problem, even though he has everything, is that he never wants to share. Even if he doesn't finish something in the cafeteria, he won't give the remainder away. He does not seem mean, but no one understands why he is so selfish – he wants everything for himself, and only for himself. So, Mateo has no friends. No one wants to play with him because he always wants the best role in the best situation. The result is that Mateo can always be found alone on a bench at recess, with his mobile phone, his candies, and his cookies. Neither the girls nor the boys want to see him. Although Mateo has everything, he is terribly bored. As an only child, he doesn't even have a brother or sister to have fun with on the weekend. And when he walks through the town to find his schoolmates, they do everything to avoid him.

seine Schulkameraden zu finden, dann tun sie alles, um ihm aus dem Weg zu gehen.

Eines Tages mitten im Schuljahr kam ein junges Mädchen namens Miranda neu in die Schule. Jeder nannte sie die Neue. Da sie niemanden kannte, näherte sie sich Mateo in der Pause. Eingeschüchtert von der Neuen, die anscheinend noch nicht bemerkt hatte, dass Mateo nichts teilte und weil er schüchtern war, konnte er ihr ein paar Süßigkeiten nicht abschlagen. Und so verliebte sich Mateo in Miranda, die wirklich seine Freundin sein wollte. Sie hatten viel Spaß zusammen und die ganze Klasse konnte nicht verstehen, warum Mateo Dinge mit Miranda teilen wollte. Sie war überhaupt nicht schüchtern, Schritt für Schritt wurde sie jedermanns Freundin. Als er bemerkte, dass seine Liebe ihn verließ, wusste Mateo nichts anderes zu tun, als sich wieder zurückzuziehen.

One day, in the middle of the year, a young girl named Miranda arrived at school. Everyone called her the newbie. Since she did not know anyone, she approached Mateo during recess. Intrigued by this new arrival who gave the impression that she hadn't noticed that Mateo did not share anything, and being timid, he was not successful in refusing her some candies. And that is how Mateo fell totally in love with Miranda, who really wanted to be his friend. They had fun together all the time and the entire class could not understand why Mateo wanted to share some things with Miranda. Since she was not shy at all, little by little, she became friends with everyone. Seeing that his love was leaving him, Mateo, not knowing what to do, preferred to return to his corner.

Er hätte nicht gedacht, dass die Rückkehr zur Einsamkeit so schwierig sein würde. Also entschied er sich, Miranda für einen Nachmittag zu sich nach Hause einzuladen. Er war ein wenig ängstlich, denn es war das erste Mal, dass er jemanden zu sich nach Hause einlud. Dieser Tag war der schönste in seinem Leben. Miranda war ein tolles Mädchen, die sich nichts aus ihrem Aussehen machte. Alles war perfekt, bis Mateo sich

entschied, ihr die Wahrheit zu sagen. Mit viel Mut erklärter er ihr, dass er Gefühle für sie hatte und fragte sie, ob sie seine Freundin sein wollte. Das überraschte Miranda nicht eine Sekunde. Als Mateo ihr eine Tour in seinem kleinen Elektrozug über das Grundstück gab, küsste ihn Miranda auf die Wange! Mateo fühlte, wie sein Herz zu rasen begann und er wurde rot.

He did not realize that the return to solitude would be so difficult. So he decided that he would invite Miranda to come to his house for an afternoon. He was a bit scared, as it was the first time that he had invited someone to his house. That day was one of the best of his life. Miranda was a really great girl who did not care about appearances. Everything was perfect, until Mateo decided to tell her the truth. With a lot of courage, he explained that he had feelings for her and asked her if she wanted to be his girlfriend. This did not surprise Miranda for one second. As Mateo gave her a tour of his property in his small electric train, Miranda kissed him on the cheek! Mateo felt his heart start to race, and he blushed.

„Ich mag dich auch sehr Mateo", sagte sie. „Ich würde wirklich gerne deine Freundin sein, aber unter einer Bedingung! Du musst von jetzt an aufhören, so egoistisch zu sein."

"Me too, I like you a lot Mateo," she said. "I would really like to become your girlfriend, but on one condition! You have to stop being selfish from this point on."

Mateo war perplex und verstand die Welt nicht mehr. Wie konnte sie nur. Er hatte alles für sie getan, sie sogar in sein Haus eingeladen!

From being on cloud nine, Mateo fell back down to earth. How dare she! He had done everything for her, even invited her to his house!

„Aber... aber...", stammelte Mateo und wusste nicht was er sagen sollte.

"But... but...," stammered Mateo, not knowing what to say.

Mateo hatte keine Zeit zum Antworten, da Mirandas Eltern kamen, um sie abzuholen. Er war wirklich traurig und gleichzeitig wütend. Er verstand nicht, warum alle von ihm wollten, dass er das weggab, was er besaß. Es gehörte doch ihm? Sie mussten einfach ihre eigenen Süßigkeiten kaufen oder? Die Tage vergingen und Mateo fand sich selbst alleine wieder. Aber dieses Mal konnte er es nicht aushalten, besonders als er bemerkte, dass Jeremy versuchte, mit Miranda zu sprechen! Er musste eine Lösung finden, ansonsten würde er nie mit Miranda zusammenkommen.

Mateo did not have the time to give a reply, as Miranda's parents had just come to pick her up. He was really sad, and, at the same time, angry. He did not understand why everyone wanted him to give away what he had. Wasn't it his, after all? They just had to buy their own candy, didn't they? Days had passed and Mateo again found himself alone. But this time, he could not take it anymore, especially when he realized that Jeremy was trying to chat up Miranda! He absolutely had to find a solution, otherwise he could never be with Miranda.

Eines Tages, als die Klasse gerade spielte, näherte er sich Miranda und fragte, ob er mitspielen könnte. Den anderen gefiel das nicht wirklich, aber Miranda bestand darauf. Am Ende des Spiels, als alle gehen wollten, rief Mateo „Wartet, wartet! Ich habe etwas für euch!" Er hatte seine größte Tüte mit Süßigkeiten mitgebracht. „Jeder nimmt sich eins!" Aber Miranda warf ihm einen Blick zu. „Ähm, ich wollte sagen drei. Jeder nimmt sich drei!", fügte er hinzu. Alle freuten sich und

Schritt für Schritt begann Mateo zu teilen. Er verteilte Kekse, Kuchen und Süßigkeiten; er verlieh seinen Gameboy und sogar seinen Scooter! Je mehr Zeit verging, umso mehr freundete er sich mit allen an.

One day, while the class was playing British Bulldogs, he approached Miranda to ask if he could play with them. The others did not really want him, but Miranda insisted. At the end of the game, while everyone was leaving, Mateo shouted, "Wait, wait! I have something for you!" He had brought with him his largest bag of candy. "Everyone take one!" But Miranda cast a glare at him. "Um, I meant to say three each!" he added. Everyone was very happy. Little by little, Mateo began to share. He gave out cookies, cake, and candies; he lent his Gameboy out, and even his scooter! The more time that passed, the more he became friends with everyone.

Als sein Geburtstag kam, lud er die ganze Klasse zu sich nach Hause ein. Seine Freunde konnten ihren Augen nicht glauben – sein Zuhause war wie ein Freizeitpark! Es war wunderbar. Alle hatten Spaß und lachten. Miranda suchte Mateo, der gerade dabei war einer Gruppe von Freunden seinen Hund vorzustellen. Sie zog ihn zu dem kleinen Elektrozug, wo er ihr erstmals seine Liebe gestanden hatte.

When his birthday arrived, he invited the entire class to have fun at his house. His friends could not believe their eyes — it was a like an amusement park! It was magnificent. Everyone had fun and laughed joyfully. Then Miranda went to find Mateo who was introducing his dog to a group of his friends. She pulled him over to the small electric train where he first pronounced his love for her.

„Siehst du, es macht mehr Spaß, wenn wir Dinge mit unseren Freunden teilen oder? ”

"So, you see that it is more fun when we share things with our friends, right?"

„Das stimmt, Miranda. Ich hätte das eher erkennen müssen", antwortete Mateo.

"It's true, Miranda, I should have realized that earlier," responded Mateo.

Miranda näherte sich ihm. Wie beim letzten Mal begann sein Herz schneller zu schlagen. Und dann küsste sie ihn auf den Mund!

Miranda then approached him. Like the last time, his heart began to beat very fast. And she gave him a kiss on the mouth!

In dem Moment gestand Mateo sich endlich selbst ein, dass wer gibt, auch etwas zurückbekommt!

At that moment, Mateo finally said to himself, that it is when we give that we receive!

Geschichte 10: Sabrina & Das Buch der Magie

Story 10: Sabrina & The Book of Magic Spells

Sabrina ist ein kleines Mädchen, das gewiss das schlimmste Benehmen an der ganzen Schule hat. Es ist nicht klug, sich mit ihr anzulegen, denn sie ist die Größte und die Stärkste. Wenn du dich jemals mit ihr anlegen solltest, dann kommt hier ein Rat: Versuche nicht gewinnen zu wollen. Denn Sabrina hasst nichts mehr als zu verlieren. Einmal, als sie Basketball auf dem Schulhof spielte, kämpfte sie mit Michael, weil ihr Team verloren hatte. Der arme Michael brach sich dabei einen Zahn aus! Das sollte dir zeigen, wie beängstigend Sabrina ist – besonders weil Michael einer der stärksten Jungen ist. Also denke daran, lass Sabrina in Ruhe und sage ja zu allem, worum sie dich bittet, klar?

Sabrina is a little girl who has, certainly, the worst attitude in the entire school. It is not smart to annoy her, as she is the biggest and the strongest. If you ever have the misfortune of playing with her, here is a word of advice: do not win at any cost. Sabrina hates losing above all else. One time, while she was playing basketball in the schoolyard, she fought with Mickael because her team lost. Poor Mickael broke a tooth! This should tell you how frightening Sabrina is — especially as Mickael is one of the strongest boys. So, remember, you have to leave Sabrina alone and say yes to whatever she asks for, is that clear?

Ich erzähle dir das, weil ich die Chance hatte, mehr als einmal schneller als sie zu sein, da ich 1.20m groß bin. Aber jetzt mache ich mich sehr klein und werde nie wieder gegen sie laufen. Mein Name ist Remy und Sabrina ist meine Schwester! Da ich sie gut kenne, warne ich alle meine Freunde nicht zu Sabrinas Feind zu werden. Nehmt euch in Acht! Aber eines Tages war Sabrina schlecht drauf und vertraute sich mir an.

I am telling you this because I had the chance more than once to run faster than her, measuring one meter twenty tall. But now, I make myself very small and will never run against her again. My name is Remy, and Sabrina is my sister! As I know her well, I warn all of my friends not to be Sabrina's enemy. Beware! But, one day, Sabrina was in an awful state and confided in me.

„Weißt du, Remy, ich habe genug davon, alle zu ängstigen! Ich möchte nicht mehr wütend sein, wenn ich so bin, dann finde ich mich selbst schrecklich!"

"You know Remy, I've had enough of making everyone scared! I don't like being angry and what's more, when I'm like that, I find myself very ugly!"

Ich wusste nicht, was ich sagen sollte, bis ich mich an die Geschichten meines Opas erinnerte. Es war die Legende der Familie, einer unser Vorfahren, der ein altes Buch mit Zaubersprüchen im Garten versteckt hatte. Sabrina dachte zuerst, ich mache Witze. Ich musste mein Lauftalent erneut unter Beweis stellen. Ich schwor ihr, dass ich nicht log. Dann suchten wir nach dem berühmten Zauberbuch, jedoch ohne viel Erfolg. Aber Sabrina wollte nicht aufgeben. Um ihre Persönlichkeit zu verändern, musste sie es auf jeden Fall finden. Nach ein paar Kämpfen und Streits fanden wir endlich das Zauberbuch. Es war im Boden einer alten Holzkiste vergraben gewesen.

I did not quite know what to say until I remembered one of my grandfather's stories. It was the legend of the family of one of our ancestors who had hidden an old book of magic spells in the garden. Sabrina thought that I was kidding at first. I had to put my running talents to the test again! I swore to her I was not lying. We then left to search for the famous spell book, but without much success. Sabrina was not going to give up. In order to change her personality, she had to find it at all costs. After a few fights and disputes, we finally found the spell book. It had been buried in the ground in an old wooden chest.

Stellt euch mal vor, wie überrascht wir waren, als wir die Schatzkarte fanden und unser Spaten heftig in Richtung der Kiste taumelte und wir begannen den Garten umzugraben, wie Archäologen, die nach Dinosaurier suchten! Das Zauberbuch war wunderbar. Der Buchband war aus Holz und goldenem Schmuck hergestellt, das hell schien. Das, was im Zauberbuch stand, war absolut fabelhaft. Es gab alle Arten von Zaubersprüchen, wie man z. B. Eine Kröte in eine weiße Taube verwandelte; wie man einen Liebeszauberspruch ausführte; wie man immer die höchste Punktzahl beim Diktat bekommt; wie man wie ein Vogel fliegen kann, dank einer Zauberfee; wo man magische Wesen im Wald finden konnte und es gab ein Haufen weiterer Formeln, Tipps und Tricks für jeden und alles.

Imagine our surprise when, having found the treasure map, our spade lurched violently towards the box and we found ourselves digging the garden like archeologists looking for dinosaurs! The spell book was magnificent. Its cover was made of wood and golden jewelry that shone brightly. What was inside the spell book was absolutely fabulous. There were all sorts of magical spells, such as how to transform a toad into a white dove, how to make a love spell, how to always get a perfect score in dictation, to fly like a bird thanks to fairy dust, where to meet magical beings in the forest, and a bunch of other formulas, tips, and tricks for anyone and anything.

Aber was Sabrina interessierte, war eine Zauberformel, die sehr speziell war. Das war die Folgende:

But what interested Sabrina was a magical formula that was very special. Here is what it said:

Beschaffe etwas Knoblauch, ein wenig Schlangenschleim und zehn sehr frische Kaninchenköttel! In einer Pfanne die erste Schicht Knoblauch, Zwiebel und Kaninchenköttel anbraten. Warte ein paar Minuten und wenn der Geruch zu stark wird, gebe ein wenig Schlangenschleim hinzu. Lasse das Ganze ruhen, decke es ab und stelle es unter den Vollmond. Decke

das Gemisch am ersten Tag des Monats auf und vermische es mit Wasser und trinke alles aus!"

Procure some garlic, some snail slime, and ten very fresh rabbit droppings! In a pan, brown the first layer of an onion, garlic, and the rabbit droppings. Wait a few minutes, and when the smell is too much, add a touch of the snail slime. Let it sit, covered, under a full moon. On the first day of the month, uncover what you've prepared, mix it with water, and drink it to the very last drop!"

Okay! Sicher ist es nicht so schlimm, wie es sich anhört! Ich weiß, dass es stimmt, denn ansonsten wäre Sabrina wütend geworden, sobald sie es getrunken hatte. Zuerst passierte nichts. Ich begann mich darauf vorzubereiten wegzulaufen, als ich den verblüfften Blick auf ihrem Gesicht sah. Aber im letzten Moment wurden Sabrinas Gesichtszüge weich und ihre Stimme wurde heller und süßer und ihr Blick war voller Liebe! Selbst ich, die Angst vor ihr hatte, gab meiner Schwester eine feste Umarmung.

Ah well! No word of a lie, it's not as bad as it seems! I know this is true because otherwise Sabrina would have been furious the moment she drank it. At first, nothing happened. I began to prepare myself to run, seeing the baffled look on her face. But at the last moment, Sabrina's facial features softened, her voice became light and dulcet, and her look was one full of love! Even I, who was scared of her, gave my sister a huge hug!

Wir schauten nicht zurück, denn sie verwandelte sich in ein sehr nettes Mädchen! Niemand an der Schule konnte das glauben. Die Kinder hatten weiterhin Angst vor ihr, bis sie erkannten, dass Sabrina wirklich nett geworden war. Es gab sogar ein Kind namens Jordan, der ihr seine Liebe gestehen wollte. Jetzt gibt es keinen Grund mehr wegzulaufen oder auf sie zu hören – Sabrina akzeptiert es zu verlieren und ist die meiste Zeit wirklich gut gelaunt.

She and I, we didn't look back and she was transformed into a very nice girl! Nobody at school could believe it! The kids continued to be scared of her until they realized that Sabrina had truly become kind. There was even a kid named Jordan who wanted to declare his love for her!

Presently, there was no need to run or to be obliging — Sabrina accepted losing and was in a really good mood.

Aber eines Tages kamen die Probleme zurück. Aus irgendeinem unbekannten Grund nutzte sich der Zauber ab und die magische Formel funktionierte nicht mehr. Während sie Badminton im Sportunterricht spielten, verlor Sabrina ihr Spiel gegen Julian. Plötzlich warf sie ihren Schläger mitten in Julians Gesicht. Panisch erinnerte er sich an einen guten Rat, den man ihm gegeben hatte, und er lief um das ganze Sportzentrum herum und rief „Hilfe! Hilfe! Helft mir!" Zuerst lachten die Kinder; sie dachten Sabrina machte irgendeinen Scherz. Aber das machte sie nur noch wütender. Ein paar Minuten später begann die ganze Klasse in alle Richtungen zu laufen. Es war ein totales Chaos. Ich versuchte mit ihr zu reden, aber das funktionierte nicht.

But one day, drama arrived. For some unknown reason, the spell wore off and the magical formula didn't work anymore. While we were playing badminton in the school gym, Sabrina lost her match against Julien. All of a sudden, she threw her racket at Julien's face. Panic stricken, he remembered an old piece of advice that I had given him, and went rushing around the entire gymnasium, yelling, "Help! Help! Help me!" At first the kids laughed; they thought Sabrina was playing a trick. But that only made her even madder. A few moments later, the entire class began to run in every direction. It was total chaos! I even tried to reason with her, but that didn't work!

Dann beruhigte sie sich. Sie war überrascht, dass die Formel nicht mehr funktionierte und so gingen wir, um nachzusehen, was das Zauberbuch sagte. Im Buch war geschrieben, dass es notwendig war, den Vorgang jeden Monat zu wiederholen. Als ich sah, was da geschrieben stand, lief ich weg, um mich vor Sabrinas Wut zu verstecken. Aber entgegen aller Erwartungen, blieb sie völlig ruhig.

Nach all diesen Abenteuern und den gelaufenen Kilometern sagte Sabrina endlich, dass sie glaubte, dass die echte Magie darin lag, wenn wir uns von selbst verändern. Und von dem Tag an wurde Sabrina sehr nett, dank ihrer eigenen Bemühungen, sich selbst zu ändern.

She eventually calmed down. Surprised that the formula did not work anymore, we left to see what the spell book said. It stipulated that it was necessary to redo the process each month. When I saw what was written, I ran away to hide from Sabrina's anger. But, against all expectations, she stayed perfectly calm. After all these adventures and the kilometers run in flight! Sabrina said she finally thinks that the real magic is when we transform ourselves on our own! And from that day on, Sabrina became very nice thanks to her own efforts to improve herself.

Conclusion

Reading is a magical activity that can transport you to wonderful places without you even having to leave your own home. We hope this book was able to do that for you. Even more, we hope you were able to improve your second language skills at the same time.

Did your reading skills in German improve as you went through the stories?

Did your listening skills get better as you listened to the audio?

Did you follow along and practice your pronunciation?

We hope you did, and we hope you had as wonderful a time with this book as we did in creating it for you. Here is a piece of advice we want to share with you:

Keep reading. It will enrich your mind and make you an even better version of yourself — better not only in school, but in life as a truly kickass individual!

Keep learning German. It will open up so many doors for you, we promise. As long as you are on your language-learning journey, we will be here to help.

Danke, Thank you

My Daily German Team

How to Download the Free Audio Files?

The audio files need to be accessed online. No worries though—it's easy!

On your computer, smartphone, iPhone/iPad, or tablet, simply go to this link:

https://mydailygerman.com/english-bedtime-audio/

Be careful! If you are going to type the URL on your browser, please make sure to enter it completely and exactly. Otherwise, it will lead you to an incorrect web page. You should be directed to a web page where you can see the cover of your book.

Below the cover, you will find two "Click here to download the audio" buttons in blue and orange color.

Option 1 (via Google Drive): The blue one will take you to a Google Drive folder. It will allow you to listen to the audio files online or download them from there. Just "Right click" on the track and click "Download." You can also download all the tracks in one click—just look for the "Download all" option.

Option 2 (direct download): The orange button/backup link will allow you to directly download all the files (in .zip format) to your computer.

Note: This is a large file. Do not open it until your browser tells you that it has completed the download successfully (usually a few minutes on a broadband connection, but if your connection is slow it could take longer).

The .zip file will be found in your "Downloads" folder unless you have changed your settings. Extract the .zip file and you will now see all the audio tracks. Save them to your preferred folder or copy them to your other devices. Please play the audio files using a music/Mp3 application.

Did you have any problems downloading the audio? If you did, feel free to send an email to support@mydailygerman.com. We'll do our best to assist you, but we would greatly appreciate it if you could thoroughly review the instructions first.

Thank you,

My Daily German Team

About My Daily German

MyDailyGerman.com believes that German can be learned almost painlessly with the help of a learning habit. Through its website and the books and audiobooks that it offers, German language learners are treated to high-quality materials that are designed to keep them motivated until they reach their language learning goals. Keep learning German and enjoy the learning process with books and audio from My Daily German.

MyDailyGerman.com is a website c reated to help busy learners learn German. It is designed to provide a fun and fresh take on learning German through:

- Helping you create a daily learning habit that you will stick to until you reach fluency, and
- Making learning German as enjoyable as possible for people of all ages.

With the help of awesome content and tried-and-tested language learning methods, My Daily German aims to be the best place on the web to learn German.

The website is continuously updated with free resources and useful materials to help you learn German. This includes grammar and vocabulary lessons plus culture topics to help you thrive in a German-speaking location—perfect not only for those who wish to learn German but also for travelers planning to visit German-speaking destinations.

For any questions, please email support@mydailygerman.com.

Your opinion counts!

If you enjoyed this book, please consider leaving a review on Amazon and help other language learners discover it.

Scan the QR code below:

OR

Visit the link below:

https://geni.us/nAHr5N

Made in the USA
Monee, IL
06 April 2024

57e477b1-f5d3-4fab-ac5e-73defb0a4df6R01